JANE BY THE BOOK

PEPPER BASHAM

To my tenderhearted son, Aaron
May you be the hero of your own story

Jane by the Book

Cover image ©2018 by Roseanna White Designs & Pepper Basham

Cover art photos ©iStockphoto.com and Pixabay used by permission.

Published in the United States of America by Pepper Basham

www.pepperdbasham.com

❀ Created with Vellum

CHAPTER 1

P redictability and order cultivate peace.
　　Jane Warwick glanced with appreciation at the great
room of the Inn at Simeon Ridge, the dying firelight in the
stone fireplace casting flickers of gold against the book-shelved walls.
Each night, with the flip of a switch, she closed out the day with a cup
of coffee in her hand before retiring to her third-story apartment.
Each night, as the firelight blinked into dying embers, after all the
many chores for the evening guests had run their courses and the
house nestled into its midnight slumber, she cradled her dainty cup
and stared into the surrounding forest's darkness.

Many people hated the great room at night, with its floor-to-
ceiling windows opening into the giant blackness of the woods and
the silhouette of the distant Blue Ridge Mountains, but Jane loved the
contented quiet after a day of hard work. She'd created the gazebo in
the back garden, sprinkling it with a garland of white fairy lights that
called her to contemplate what she never did during the daytime
hours. Love. Romance. A hero-waiting-to-be-found...or even better,
find her.

Twilight provided a safe place for introspection, freedom for her
heart to access a world she'd distanced herself from for four years.

But only in these untouched moments of the evening, after most of the guests had retired to their cozy suites on the first two floors of the century-old B&B. She stared at the glittering gazebo, all magical in the moonlight, and wondered if her future would look more like the shine of the gazebo or the darkness of the surrounding forest? If the past set a precedent on the future? She pinched her eyes closed to the thought.

The gazebo lights flickered then dimmed, as if in morbid reply. She checked her watch. Midnight. Time for the carriage to transform back into a pumpkin. Time to call it a day.

She carried her cup to the doorway and turned back to the room, flipping off the light. Moonlight poured through the windows and bathed the oak hardwoods with a pale sheen. Everything looked in perfect order for the guests to enjoy their morning coffee and appreciate the unending view of mountains. She smiled.

She'd found her place. Four years had seen her move from heartbroken bride to housekeeping manager at the inn, an occupation she didn't know would suit her niche for organization and order so well. Her best friend, Nora, had known. Pulling her from her jilted heap on the stone church floor, Nora had given Jane's pitiful fingers work to do and, in turn, created an occupation she'd grown to adore. Service. Order. Four years of a perfectly predictable routine and the natural reward of a job well done. Satisfaction.

She took the three flights of stairs up to her apartment, her body weary from coordinating the details of the massive inn to the folded serviettes on the restaurant tables. The red- and gold-mingled carpet runner, stretching the length of the narrow hallway at the top of the stairs, hushed the clip of her sling-backs as she pulled her key ring from the pocket of her apron and opened her door. The sweet mist of apple blossom enveloped her, drawing her into the haven of rooms she'd called home ever since she began working at the inn. Three rooms and a bath. A living area, an office, and her bedroom. Small, tidy, and free of charge. All she needed.

"I knew you'd still be awake."

Jane rushed inside her room at the sound of the voice. She

pressed against the door and almost succeeded in closing the distance without another interruption to her day.

Nora Simeon squeezed through the gap just before the door snipped closed.

Jane leaned back against the closed door as her friend rushed in, face a bundle of smiles. "Are you just getting in from Charlotte?"

Nora's cheeks took on that rosy glow of romance, eyes even sparkling like the fairy-lights on the gazebo. "Ethan's been up here to visit me the last three times, so it's the least I could do."

Jane sat down on her red loveseat and tugged off her shoes. "Sounds serious."

Nora's grin brightened as she collapsed into a navy armchair that complimented Jane's throw pillows on the love seat. "He's so...well, wonderful. We fit, you know? Same dreams, same goals, same faith, and..." She scooched to the edge of the chair and entwined her fingers, her eyes gleaming with mischief.

She knew that look. Trouble. Probably at Jane's expense. The first three notes of Beethoven's Fifth played a warning theme in Jane's mind.

"You're going to go with me and Ethan to England, right?"

Jane rubbed a palm to her forehead. "I have a lot to do here."

"And you've done such a great job training Gwyn. Simeon Ridge will still be standing when you return." Nora raised a brow. "Come on, Jane. This is Ethan's first inn all on his own and he needs the best to get his staff in tip-top shape. I'm going along to help with designs."

"And to spend time with Ethan."

Her grin shone, and she scrunched up her shoulders. "Icing on the cake." She sighed and refocused from whatever daydream Ethan's name inspired in her head. "It's also a chance for you to really stretch yourself, travel..." Nora's gaze traveled across the room. "Visit the land of your forefathers and uncover that little mystery you keep locked in your heirloom desk?"

Jane's attention shot to the 1842 mahogany roll top in the corner of the room—the one piece of furniture her grandfather made certain went to the family namesake. Jane. Her face lost its warmth a little.

Leave her job? Travel abroad? She pressed her palm to her stomach and drew a deep breath. England was across an ocean!

"I think you can train the staff for Ethan's new inn on your own. After all, you're part owner of this place." She waved around the room, trying to think up more excuses. She'd never been a fan of change, but when Emory left her at the altar, something closed inside of her. This little haven of the world helped her heal, hid her from the stares in the streets. She'd grown here, proven herself strong and smart. She *knew* the plan for The Inn and Simeon Ridge and the family who owned it. "You already know all you need to train any staff members, on this side of the Pond or the next."

Nora shook her long, glossy brown hair. Her locks lay along her back in perfect waves, unlike Jane's unruly blond mess, which was often pinned back or flipped up out of the way. "Don't even try that with me. You know as well as I do that I'm more of the big picture person around here, and you are Miss Details. That's what Ethan is going to need for these new hires, and he's willing to *pay your way to England*." Her eyes widened in a 'don't be stupid' reminder. "Nearly three weeks. In Bath, England. For free."

"Fine." Jane sighed, tamping down a twinge of excitement for later. "I'll start making arrangements with Gwynn and Liam tomorrow morning, so they'll know what to cover in my absence."

"Perfect." Nora pushed herself up from the chair and sauntered to the door, her grin much too crooked to leave Jane in peace over their upcoming trip. "We leave on Thursday."

Jane shot to her feet. "That's only four days away."

"I told you about the trip a month ago." Nora shrugged, opening the door like the escapee she was. "It's not my fault you waited until the last minute to finally agree to come."

Jane launched a throw pillow from the couch at Nora's retreating back but only received a trail of light laughter in response as the door closed and the pillow landed two feet from the threshold. She groaned and retrieved the pillow, fluffing it until it lay just so in its usual place at the corner of her loveseat.

England. Her gaze shifted back to the desk and her feet followed the course as if pulled by an imaginary string attached to great, great, great...Jane Ridley. The one Jane in the family line who never married. Or had she? She'd obviously had kids, if Jane was a direct descendant, but no one in the family had ever been able to find out what happened to her.

Jane rolled up the top of the desk and pulled open a large drawer, in the far-right top corner. A unique knob that looked something like a silver daisy in bloom, the only one of its kind on the desk, decorated its front. She housed one item in that drawer—a stained, yellow-paged journal enclosed in a Ziploc bag. What secrets hid behind that solitary daisy knob? What family mysteries lay embedded in Granny Jane's journal?

Her journal ended at an abrupt place and without an answer. Jane touched the bag, almost afraid to draw the journal out, but her fingers craved the connection. The beauty in the story-without-an-ending.

Had Granny Jane been willing to risk everything for love and an uncertain future? Or had she taken the sensible route and remained in the comfortable life she'd made for herself?

The question rushed into the present as if nudging Jane's own consideration. Jane curled her fingers into her palm and closed the desk. Why should what have happened to Granny Jane matter to her, over a hundred and fifty years in the past? It shouldn't.

Jane stepped back and shook her head. She'd believe what she'd always believed, refuse the romance and continue with her sensible life. The practical thing.

She nodded. Romance wasn't a risk she planned to take. Just like Granny Jane hadn't.

WHY DID women have to be like a Chinese finger puzzle?

Titus Stewart stared at the blank page of his laptop and willed his heroine to come alive. Even fictional women presented dilemmas large enough to reach into his discombobulated life and send him reeling for mental cover. He squinted at the screen. Well, this time he *had* to succeed. His editor wouldn't accept another failure.

He placed his hand on his chin and gazed out the train window, the green English countryside passing in a blur of rock-fenced pastures dotted with sheep, a field stone church breaking through the tree line, and a smattering of disconnected buildings from a variety of eras. Crimson, goldenrod, and russet light pierced the low-hanging mist that decorated the mid-November afternoon. If only the incomparable beauty of the day could sink into his inspiration and create a novel to launch his career out of the literary doldrums...or worse, his editor's threats.

Wait. What had he said about low-hanging mist in crimson?

He blinked and frantically typed out the sentence. The words might not work for the plotline battling in his mind, but the sentence deserved remembrance. His grin broadened, and he looked back out the window. He loved England. It was in his bloodline through generations and never failed to inspire his creativity.

Which was exactly what he needed.

Having a friend with a high-class inn in the area only made the journey to England better. That Ethan gave him a discounted rate fit right in with Titus's writing budget. His lips took a slight curl. He'd been trying to figure out where he was going to place Detective Jack Miracle next, and circumstances had given him the clues he needed. Miracle's next mystery would happen somewhere among Bath's iconic buildings and cobblestone streets.

Now all he needed was a plot and mystery to entertain his readers and a strong heroine to keep Miracle in check over a period of three books...or more. Titus couldn't even imagine creating a solid heroine for one book, let alone three.

Oh God, give me inspiration!

Titus's eyes drifted to the single line of text blotting his computer screen. Well, written drivel was better than no drivel at all, though his editor gave little wiggle room for words that didn't advance his story. Despite reviews that praised the plot of the last novel in his Detective Jack Miracle series, critics and readers alike criticized its character development, including the heroine's. Titus *had* to change his methods. He sighed and leaned his head back against the seat, but his mind refused to focus on finding a solution to his heroine debacle. He closed the laptop and pulled out his notebook, fingering the detritus crowding his bag until he found his favorite writing utensil. He thought—and wrote—better with a pen in hand.

Writing female characters always had been difficult for him, something Ethan would say reflected Titus's eclectic and somewhat disgruntled romantic life, but honestly, Titus *cared* too much in relationships. He jumped all in from the start and terrified women.

He needed to be more like Detective Miracle. Suave. Aloof.

Women liked that in men, didn't they? All broody and Darcy-ish.

Or, at least, he consoled himself with such ideas. Maybe his thinking was drivel too.

Drivel.

What a wonderful word.

Focus, Titus. He needed a name for the heroine. His editor wanted a consistent female fixture in Jack's life, and Titus had decided she'd most likely be English since Jack hailed from England himself.

Names...names.

Beatrice? Decidedly English and creative. A well-known name in the Lake District. He chuckled. Maybe the heroine is a famous author who also draws bunnies that talk?

He rolled his gaze heavenward, begging for help again.

Clara? Beautiful name but he'd written a murdering Clara in the second book of the series and doubted Jack had the heart to handle another one in his life.

Lydia? He grinned. Yes, Lydia. He wrote the name down on his paper. Lydia Whitby.

And what did she do?

"Yes!" His exclamation garnered attention from a few people sitting nearby. He offered them an apologetic grin. "I just met my heroine."

His elderly seatmate's silver brows rose to his receding hairline.

Titus scrawled out the idea. *Secretary to Lord Atticus Ramsey.* Jack's great uncle who had been like a father to him. Yes, she'd be a constant fixture in Jack's life for certain, which would make her easy to bring into future stories.

If this idea worked.

Titus searched the train car for ideas about Lydia's appearance. What would a secretary in 1912 look like? A smart, efficient, attractive secretary at that.

Women liked strong females. So did he, as a matter of fact. They just didn't usually like him.

A purple-haired teen sat in front of him, black nails typing away on her mobile. Definitely not early 1900s appropriate. His gaze drifted to a white-haired woman with a book almost raised to her nose. He squinted to make out the title. Ah, mystery. Good choice. His attention pulled toward two women at the front of the train car. The one with long, loose brown hair moved her hands as she talked in an animated way, clearly excited about whatever the other woman held in her hands. Pretty.

But was she Lydia Whitby?

He wasn't feeling it.

The lady next to the animated one wore her blond hair in a tight ponytail, highlighting a long slender neck above the collar of her black coat. A profile of a high cheekbone and...hmm... could those be black-framed glasses? Very studious-looking. She smiled. A small smile. Controlled. Guarded.

His grin began its climb. Nice to meet you, Miss Lydia Whitby.

He scrawled down his observations with some added conjectures. After all, he was writing a fictional character and could take liberties. Conservative. Organized. A bit snippy. Pouty mouth and... Eyes. That's where he needed a defining characteristic. His heroine could control everything except those eyes. Even their color needed to be unique.

Green. Not hazel but a pure, bright green. And she probably didn't like how noticeable they were.

He chuckled, gathering a few more curious looks, and eased into his seat, continuing to watch the blonde in the black coat. The other lady did most of the talking, but his muse? She remained quiet. What did she look like? Would she let him take a photo of her?

Memory stung a clear reminder into his cheek, and he rubbed his face at the unwelcome recollection. Maybe asking her for a photo wasn't the best option. His frown deepened. He could try to get in front of her long enough to see her face, but that would only happen if she disembarked in Bath too.

With his luck, she was probably traveling all the way to Bristol.

The two friends moved closer together, the brunette's eyes widening as she stared at a piece of paper between them. Was it a book? He sat up. Yellowed pages. Nondescript binding.

Was Lydia Whitby a book collector? Or even better, a book thief?

He shook his imagination into order just as the train slowed for his stop. Maybe he could walk close enough to see her face *and* her book as he disembarked. Or he'd just look like the good-natured stalker he was.

She shifted ahead of him. Heaven and earth, she was gathering her belongings! His gaze shot heavenward in an unfettered internal shout of thanksgiving. He rushed to finish collecting his luggage, stuffed his notepad inside his coat pocket, and slung his computer case over his shoulder.

Miss Whitby traveled light, unlike her friend, who despite two rolling bags, a carry on, and a purse still navigated the train without stumbling in the aisle or knocking into other passengers. How did women do that?

Wait! He was a gentleman.

He hurried ahead just as the ladies came to the doors, and Miss Whitby's friend's bag caught on the gap between the train and the station floor.

"Let me help with that."

The brunette looked up. "Oh, thank you." She shrugged an apology. "I may have overdone my packing this time."

"It's hard to know what the weather will be like this time of year." He tugged her bag free and followed the pair, finally catching Miss Whitby's attention. Green! Her eyes were green! Not dark green like a pine tree but more of a spring green. She walked ahead, attempting to place the old book back into some protective bag. Good idea. Wouldn't want to lose a stolen book.

Maybe she was a book thief.

But then, why would she have it out in broad daylight?

"You're American?" Miss Whitby's friend's eyes widened as she awaited his answer.

"Yes." He jerked his attention away from Miss Whitby's skeptical expression and into the brunette's welcome one. "As are you."

She laughed and stepped through the station checkout, but Miss Whitby didn't share so much as a smile. Maybe she was more than a little snippy. As he pulled the luggage through the tight spaces, keeping his computer bag from catching the corners and his mind on Miss Whitby's possible quirks, he didn't notice that the women had stopped to allow a wheelchair to pass until it was too late.

He bumped into the friendly brunette, who fell into Miss Whitby, whose forward motion sent bags and pages flying in all directions. His stomach dropped. Pages flying? He'd had the exact same thing happen with a final manuscript draft two years ago. It was one of the worst moments of his life.

Besides his decision to shave his legs and chest hair on some stupid fraternity dare. He cringed at the memory and dropped his bags in a mad dash for the runaway papers. No one should face anything close to his manuscript disaster or his self-skinning. Ever.

Miss Whitby ran off into one direction after the flying paper tornado and her darker-haired cohort ran in another. He snatched at one of the pages. Stamped another into place on the sidewalk. Untangled another from a bicycle tire. The antiquated writing distracted him from furthering his rescue mission. *October 14, 1856.* What?

I must let him go. His world and mine are incompatible in every way.

"Thank you." Miss Whitby peeled the paper from his fingers, her green gaze blazing into his.

Well, this wasn't the way he'd hoped to gain her attention.

"What... What is that?"

She placed the paper within the folds of the antique binding, her fingers focused on the yellow pages, her eyes turned away from his. "A family heirloom." She dashed off for a paper floating through the air, and he rescued another one before a car ran over it, resulting in a blaring horn and dirty look sent his way.

He took his time walking toward snippy Miss Whitby so he could look over the words. *Edwin has been promoted to captain. After three years, he has finally been promoted to captain of his own ship. His letters fairly beam with his plans for us, plans I cannot share with Mother or Father. To them, he will always be the poor merchant's son, but to me...*

"Thank you for retrieving yet another one."

Titus held to the page until she looked up at him. Why was it so difficult for her to meet his gaze? "Would you mind telling me your name, so I'll stop calling you Miss Whitby in my head?"

She blinked, tilted her head to examine him, and blinked again while still holding to one edge of the page. "Why would you..." She shook her head. "Jane?"

"Are you sure?" His grin widened, and he released the paper.

"Jane!" The brunette ran toward them. "I found a few more, all from the same month of the journal entry."

"Journal entry? From the mid-eighteen hundreds?" Titus tried to peer over Jane's shoulder to see more of the pages, but she slipped them into the binding.

"And with your help I almost lost them." Her gaze trailed down him and back, an exhausted sigh pulling at her shoulders.

He stood up straighter to see if a few extra inches might increase her interest. Nope. "Listen here, it was an accident. You shouldn't have had pages that old out in the open where anything could happen to them anyway."

She narrowed her green eyes into slits, and his nose tingled with the sting of thoughts she failed to voice. Without another word, she turned, grabbed her bags, and marched down the street to a waiting car.

Yep. She was Lydia Whitby. Titus ran his hands through his hair, considering the latest predicament with his heroine. As he watched Miss Whitby—*Lydia*—enter the car, he couldn't imagine Detective

Miracle finding anything interesting about his newest romance. Well, except for those green eyes and long legs.

But what did he know? He was just the author. The characters ended up doing what they wanted anyway.

A familiar form stepped from the driver's side of the ladies' waiting car and waved at Titus. He squinted. Ethan? Poor guy, they'd just had lunch in Charlotte a few days ago. The man was a world-traveling expert now.

Titus' attention switched back to the ladies. A bubble of laughter formed in the back of his throat. No way. Ethan had mentioned in their phone call before the trip that he was bringing his fiancé and her best friend to stay at the Elliott Elizabeth Inn for a few weeks.

Nora. He grabbed his bags and walked toward the car. And Jane.

Well, well... Maybe some live character development was exactly what he needed.

CHAPTER 2

Jane's gaze flashed to the paper-snatching stranger to Ethan and back again. Why was Nora's boyfriend flagging down the lunatic who'd almost destroyed her family heirloom? Her anger hitched on the obvious— she hadn't placed the journal into her bag before disembarking, so the situation could *partially* be construed as her fault, but the crazy man clearly had two left-feet and a little too much curiosity.

His wild pale-blue eyes that had so intently searched hers moments before left a strange imprint on Jane's mind. He'd stared at her as if trying to read all the way into her childhood.

No wonder he'd looked away. There wasn't much to see. Or at least not many good things.

She shrugged off the residual tingle of the memory and turned her frustration to the man sauntering toward the car.

"You've met Nora already?" Ethan took the stranger's outstretched hand. The man smiled, the kind of smile that took over his whole face. Genuine. No-holds-barred. A little too unreserved for Jane's comfort.

The stranger looked between the two women until his attention landed on Nora. "I thought you looked familiar. I should have recognized you from the photos Ethan posts in every social media outlet known to man. You've inspired him to participate online instead of just lurk. I should thank you. This way I know when he's actually *in* the country."

Ethan laughed, a warm sound Jane had come to appreciate in Nora's prince charming. It had been a long time since she'd seen her friend so happy. A twinge hitched in Jane's chest. Not jealousy but... something. Longing? Sadness? Whatever it was, she pushed the idea down and turned her glare back to the stranger.

"It's because Nora looks so great in photos." Ethan took Nora's hand in his and squeezed her fingers with a gentle touch. "I may as well share them."

Nora's smile grew to Disney princess proportions, and she slid her arm around Ethan, kissing him on the cheek. "I think you're awfully cute too." She turned to the stranger. "And I can't believe I didn't recognize you from photos either. Titus Stewart!" Without hesitation she took him into her arms as if she'd grown up with the guy.

Jane's southern sensibilities, though, didn't run *that* deep. She'd leave hugging complete strangers to Nora's seventh-generation North Carolina background. The staunch British genes in Jane's veins kept her hands to herself, especially from strangers who called her the wrong name 'in his head'? She studied him. What sort of name was Titus, anyway?

"It's so nice to finally meet you! Ethan's told me so many stories about the two of you in high school and college."

Titus's eyes took on a cartoonish glimmer. Childlike. Devilish in a harmless manner. What was going on in his mind behind that smile? Jane looked away. She didn't want to know.

"I hope he only told you the *really* good ones. Stories aren't worth telling unless they're really good."

"I hear yours are, but I've not had a chance to read one yet." Nora turned her eyes downward, and a blush crept into her cheeks. "I will though! I love historical fiction."

"Well, I'm hoping to only make them better." Titus shrugged, the humble tilt to his chin doing wonders for his attractiveness. His gaze flipped to Jane, an intense look of knowing that sent her insides crawling with uncertainty. She pinched the car door as it stood open, wishing she could disappear inside. Without one bit of awkwardness, Titus stepped forward, a hand outstretched in enthusiastic welcome. "And who may you be, besides the owner of a small literary treasure?"

His greeting paused her response. "J...Jane."

His brow crinkled, confused. "Jane? You said that before, but is it just Jane?"

She nodded, trying to sort out this guy. "Yes, just Jane."

He tilted his head and studied her. "So, what is your middle name?"

Her bottom lip loosed without a response. Her middle name? "I... I don't see why—"

His head tilted the other direction, hair flipping to the same side, reminding her a little of a curious floppy-eared dog. "You just don't remind me of a Jane."

"What? I don't look like a Jane?"

"Not that exactly." He narrowed his eyes to get a better look at his specimen. Jane leaned away. "You have this elegance to you, which should be reflected in a character's...um...a person's name, I think. I bet your middle name makes up for it."

She hated her middle name. "You're a strange person, Mr. Stewart."

His grin crooked and a strange zing shot through her middle at the sight. "I get that a lot."

"Cecily. My middle name is Cecily."

He slapped his hands together and laughed, rocking back on his feet. "That's excellent. Now that fits much better."

Jane looked to Ethan then Nora, attempting to find some interpretation for the man's odd behavior.

"He's an author, Jane." Ethan shook his head, walked to the back of the car, and added the luggage to the boot. "He's always assigning names to imaginary and real people. The first time he saw a photo of Nora, he said she looked more like an Evangeline."

Nora's laugh lilted into the conversation. "Oh, I remember you telling me that, though I have to argue with the elegance of the name Jane, Titus. After all, we are in Jane Austen territory."

"You don't want to mess with her and Jane Austen, Titus." Ethan stood behind Nora, shaking his head and sliding a palm beneath his chin in warning. "Life-threatening stuff."

Jane grinned. Nora's passion for the classic author came through with hilarious eccentricity. She'd even dressed in costume, complete with an almost-homicidal-bonnet, to attend the Jane Austen Festival a few months earlier. *Full costume.*

"Right!" Titus's palms raised in surrender. "I'm a big fan of authors and writing and stories, so the spirit of Jane Austen can feel perfectly safe with my glowing admiration."

Nora's laugh returned, and she handed her final bag to Ethan. "Good because I really want us to be friends, Titus, and hating on Jane Austen is a definite friend-killer."

Ethan finished with the bags and gestured toward the car. "I can't wait to show you my inn. She's beautiful, thanks to Nora's expert design-eye, and I'm thrilled to have your help, Jane. I have a mixed staff, but mostly new people, and since the Elliott Elizabeth Inn is going to be run more like a B&B than one of my father's hotels, I want my staff to be trained in that vein. More relaxed and personal."

Jane felt her eyebrow rise. Personal? Relaxed? She drew in a deep breath and envisioned the massive rooms of the Inn at Simeon Ridge – the rustic elegance and classic charm. Was it possible to bring such a feeling into a decidedly British culture? The inn would give her a clue, once they got there.

Her gaze shifted to Nora's as her best friend walked around the car, mentally begging her to trade spots with Mr. Odd Author who had better hair than Jane did. Not as long as hers but with fantastic volume on top. Nora's lovestruck gaze fastened on Ethan and never noticed Jane's desperation. What could she expect? Nora's brain was filled with Austen, Ethan, and the power of true love. Who could compete?

Jane curbed her smile at Nora's fairytale happiness and slipped into the back seat with Titus beside her. His satchel bag spilled over the clear separation line woven into the seat between them and he took up much more room than she'd expected. She pressed into the door to give him – and especially her - plenty of space.

Calm down, Jane. If he's a friend of Ethan's... She frowned. Would the wounds ever heal completely? Ever. Already Titus took up too much space in her head. She didn't need him to crowd into her physical existence too.

"So, Jane Cecily, what is the journal all about?"

She took a deep breath and turned to Titus, attempting to start afresh with the man who'd nearly destroyed her family heirloom, not to mention found her name deficient in some way. "It's a journal of my ancestor's that's been passed down through the generations."

"Since the mid-eighteen hundreds?"

Those pale eyes, so wide with wonder like a child's, held hers. "Yes. We've been careful to preserve it." Unlike today. She winced at her own part in the debacle and looked away, pulling with care the old book from the plastic bag that housed it in her purse. The place she *should* have had it when they were on the train.

"What Jane isn't divulging, Titus"—Nora turned from her position in the front seat and offered a mischievous eyebrow wiggle— "is that the journal was written by one Jane Ridley, who had an unrequited romance with a merchant sailor."

"Nora." Jane tried to close Nora's mouth with a solid stare. "I'm sure Mr. Stewart doesn't want to hear about my family stories."

"Don't be too sure about that, Jane." Ethan laughed from the driver's seat. "Titus has used his family history to inspire his fiction."

"Oh, right!" Nora turned to see Jane. "Historical detective novels. Right Titus?"

"Yeah."

"And they're based on family history?" Jane attempted to keep too much curiosity from her voice, but she couldn't stop her gaze from studying him with a little renewed interest. Not too much, but enough to engage in small-talk until they reached the inn.

He cleared his throat and tugged at the edge of his jacket. Was he uncomfortable talking about himself? Why didn't that fit for some reason? "I don't have anything as tangible and interesting as a journal to draw from." He waved toward the book in her hands, and she diverted her attention from his face to the pages, reordering them as she listened. "Just stories passed down from my grandfather about his father. He was the second son of an earl who lost his estate at the time around World War I when a lot of English aristocrats had to downsize. What inheritance he received after all the debts were paid, he used to buy a country house in Cambria." His hands moved as he talked, adding to his energetic-person. "The Lake District. Amazing place. Anyway, he took up the hobby of sleuthing. Seemed to be pretty good at it too."

"So they're true stories?" Jane peeked at him from her periphery. "About this detective grandfather of yours?"

Titus laughed, a sound as free as Nora's. "I wish. They'd probably be much higher on the bestsellers list if they *were* true. Truth is more outrageous than fiction, as a rule." He grinned and pierced her with another blast of pale blue. "I take what stories I *do* know about Grandpa Jack and fictionalize the rest. He must have been good at what he did because he left enough money behind, so we've been able to keep up his house in Cambria for all these years without selling. In fact, once I leave Bath, I'm headed there to celebrate the holidays with my family."

Family. Jane's fingers stilled on the papers. She had an uncle and aunt in Georgia, but she wasn't too certain they fit her definition of 'family.' They'd shared some summer vacations and a few holiday celebrations, but life and distance only deepened the disconnected groove of her disconnected family. Nora's family had become more of one to her, taking her with them on vacations, spending holidays together.

"Do you make a living from your writing, Titus? Like J.K. Rowling or Stephen King?" This from Nora.

"Oh no! I'll need to write a lot more stories and build a bigger fan base to even consider that possibility, but for now, just the pleasure of writing is enough."

His easy-friendliness and undemanding conversation loosened the tension in Jane's spine. "So...so what do you do for a living?"

"I create and design story worlds for video games."

Oh man, so this guy was just a big kid. That fit much better in her mind. She examined him. Video games for someone in his late twenties, perhaps. Now she could at least feel sorry for him, but somehow, she didn't. The weird combination of Titus Stewart seemed to fit as much as his unpredictable hair. "That sounds interesting." She forced a smile and continued adjusting the journal papers.

"You say that like my parents did when my brother and I first started the business, but after five years, my coworkers and I bring in a steady income and still love what we do. You know? Feeds the creativity and the heart. Is your job like that for you? Inspiring?"

Jane smoothed her palm over one of the pages, avoiding eye contact and the prick of his question. She enjoyed making the world more efficient and ordered, but inspiring?

"She's amazing, Titus. She can take the most complex guest situations or even catastrophes and somehow fix them, so that everyone is content with the results." Nora smiled and sighed into her seat. "She completely reworked the space at Simeon Ridge to make the B&B more user-friendly."

"That's what I'm counting on for Elliott Elizabeth."

Jane breathed in their confidence and hoped Ethan's inn proved as predictable as Simeon Ridge. The car took an incline, and Jane shifted the papers in her lap, her gaze taking in a discrepancy. "Oh no!" She shifted through the pages. "Three pages are missing." Was that Jane's voice? Did she really sound so pathetic?

"You have them memorized?"

She singed Mr. Floppy hair with another glare. She refused to divulge that she'd read this journal over fifty times, especially after Emory left her at the altar. "Not all of them." She exaggerated her eye roll for his benefit. "But I *know* this one. It's one of the last entries before Jane Ridley disappears from history."

"We can go back later to look for them," Nora offered with her usual optimism.

The horizon gave off a dusky hue. "We couldn't find them in daylight. How on earth will we locate them in the dark?"

"Do you think you can recall what they said and rewrite those pages?" Titus pulled a pen from his jacket pocket. "You dictate, even, and I'll write."

Jane opened her mouth to reply, but the magnificent three-story building emerging before them distracted her from responding. *This* was the Elliott Elizabeth Inn? Jane had imagined a shift between two extremes—a cottage inn or a modern high rise—but this beautiful, historic Georgian structure stood like a time capsule of sandstone and character. Two pairs of dark mahogany doors waited beneath a curved portico of matching stonework. Jane envisioned two massive ornate flower pots on either side of the doorways, a bright welcome to the inn's already magnificent entrance.

"Ethan, it's even better than your photos, man." Titus opened the door before the car had rolled to a stop. "I think it's a perfect place for a murder."

Jane shot a look over the top of the car to the crazy man. He met her shock with a wink. "Fictionally speaking."

A strange tremor started at the pit of her stomach and branched into an explosion of heat in her face. Oh no, no! She would *not* feel attraction from someone as unpredictable as Titus Stewart.

"Just wait, Titus. When I take you on a tour and give you some of the history I've discovered about this place, you'll have enough story fodder for three more books." Ethan opened the trunk and gestured for two men wearing red coats who waited at the front door. "Take this luggage"—he pointed to Jane's and Nora's— "to the Elizabeth suite, please." He waved toward Titus's. "And these will go to the Darcy suite."

Jane flipped her attention to Ethan. If the names of the suites followed the natural pairing in Austen, then they were all housed near each other. Her shoulders drooped in complete defeat. How would she steer clear of Titus now?

"Remember what I told you about the Elliott Elizabeth Inn in Bath?" Nora linked her arm through Jane's, sprinkling the discomforting moment with sunshine. "It celebrates all things Jane Austen. Ethan even renamed the rooms after characters in her books."

Jane nudged her friend. "Your dream-come-true-palace."

"Exactly." Nora laughed. "And if the theme-based idea works, Ethan plans to expand in more places than just Bath and Yorkshire. It's all very exciting."

Jane looked back at the beautiful building. *And almost magical.*

"And I saved the best two suites, top floor, for us." Ethan nodded toward the third-floor windows. "Guys in the Darcy suite. Ladies in the Lizzie suite." He grinned at Nora. "Right across the hall from each other the whole time you're here." He smiled at Jane and Titus. "Imagine what good friends we'll all become by then."

Jane's gaze fastened on Titus, whose smile only widened. "Maybe we can uncover your story, Jane Cecily?"

She looked from the infuriating man back to the third-floor windows of the inn. *Dear Lord, help her.* The only plot she wanted Titus Stewart to uncover was the one that kept his curiosity far away from her family heirloom and his smile as far from the Elizabeth suite as the Darcy suite allowed.

She sighed and tugged her bag up on her shoulder, trying to shake his 'fine eyes' from her mind and think of a way to keep Titus Stewart uninterested in Jane Ridley or her story. Otherwise, this was going to be a very long visit.

CHAPTER 3

J ane Cecily Warwick.

Titus followed the cobblestone sidewalk through the main part of Bath, the descent toward the train station a pleasant step back into time—a quieter era with market vendors and welcome smiles ushering in the morning. The creamy limestone of hundreds of buildings scattered in all directions, peppering the skyline. He grinned. Bath was a little different than his home outside Charlotte, North Carolina. Though the buildings lining the street in Bath were centuries older than the Mayberryesque appeal of home, a quaint, welcoming feel buffered the air of this city long associated with Jane Austen and Roman-built baths.

His thoughts turned back to Jane, or Lydia, as he referred to her in his mind. Ah, yes, Detective Jack Miracle would find her quite the enigma. An attractive enigma but certainly not one for romance at first. She kept her emotions closed off from others. Quiet. Disciplined. Cautious. Jack would probably feel annoyance at her prudishness at first, but then his natural curiosity would compel him to discover what hid behind the unexpected glimmer in those moss-green eyes.

Jack couldn't help it. If there was a mystery to solve, even the smallest curiosity, he had to uncover the answer, but Lydia Whitby... Titus grinned. She wasn't going to make it easy on the detective. No siree. Jane's disappointed expression flickered across his mind as he crossed the street in front of the train station in pursuit of the missing journal pages. Only a few people waited outside the station, talking in small groups or reading a newspaper at a distance from the station doors. He shoved his hands in his pockets and scanned the area, pushing aside the realization that his search-and-rescue operation would likely lead to nothing.

No, he wouldn't admit defeat. His grin hitched, and he straightened his spine. He'd take notes from the clever Detective Jack Miracle. Now, what would Jack do?

First, he'd observe then he'd attempt to recreate the scene of the crime. Titus paused and took in the entire front section of the station, investigating one corner to the next. Halfway across the front of the station, underneath the awning, he discovered one of the pages crumpled behind the Bath Spa signage. Somehow, the wind had carried the page and wedged the faded white paper behind the dirty white sign. No wonder it had been difficult to see.

Titus smoothed the paper against the front of his jacket and peered down at the script. His fingers tingled from the very idea that the page was over one hundred years old.

How can I think of marrying him? Father has opposed the match since our first meeting and now, as I look to a future paved for me by expectation and the desires of my own mind, how can I imagine relinquishing it all for the sake of my heart? The heart is unreliable. Its instability beats against what my mind has purposed for years...what my parents have cultivated within me. Oh, unsteady heart! Why won't you forget the kindness in his voice and the passion in his prayers? His world is one unknown to you! Relinquish this hold on him so that you can walk freely into the future you've planned. Give him his Cecily with a free heart.

"Pardon me." A woman's voice pierced into Titus's focus, and he realized he was blocking the entrance into the station.

"Oh, I'm sorry." He slid away and folded the paper, his feet faltering back a step. He'd stumbled upon a real-life mystery. Is this what Jack felt like? The thrill? The anticipation? Was Cecily 'the other woman'? Titus's fingers itched for his keyboard, to pour out the emotions behind his experience into his fictional world, but he continued his search. Jane Cecily needed her heirloom.

Recreate the scene of the crime.

He retraced his steps as far as the ticket master would allow then walked out of the station, searching the area for any sign of a paper. Three times he repeated his movements.

"What are you doing?"

Titus turned to the ticket master and shrugged. "I lost something yesterday, and I'm trying to find it."

The man eyed him with skepticism, an expression Titus knew well. It translated from America to England without one missed interpretation. People really needed more imagination, as a whole.

"We got a lost and found, you know."

Titus followed the direction of the man's thick finger to a small window on the opposite side of the station. "You're brilliant!"

The man shook his head and went back to his work, but Titus dashed toward the window. Halfway through his animated detailing of the previous day's events, the elderly clerk raised her palm. "If you'd just asked for an old letter, I'd have given it to you. No need for the full story."

Titus frowned then forced a smile as the woman handed him the paper. He hated the sting of an unfinished tale, always had. His grandpa encouraged the love of storytelling with his quite unbeliev-able tales of family history, but it was his grandmother who really encouraged the hunt for a mystery. Even as a little boy, she'd take him on excursions in the backyard for hidden treasures like...turtles and four-leaf clovers. "Was this the only one?"

She nodded. "And it was lucky that one got turned in. Doesn't look like more than rubbish but someone noticed the handwriting and thought it may be special."

"Oh, it is!" His face relaxed with more authenticity. "You've been a great deal of help."

The woman smiled. "What's so important about the note, then?"

CHAPTER 3 | 25

He shrugged. "I'm not sure but I think the woman it belongs to will be very happy to have it returned to her." He waved the page at her. "If you find one more like this, would you keep it, please? I'll check back tomorrow."

The woman chuckled and shook her silvery head. "It's a miracle someone turned in that one, but *if* I do find another, I'll hold it for you here."

"Excellent." He tapped the counter and turned to leave.

"You're determined enough, aren't you?" She shook her head again. "I suspect if anyone will find it, you will."

Titus straightened his posture and grinned at the clerk. Yes, he'd done enough sleuthing research to take on a little adventure in the real world, enough to make granny proud and inspire a semi-toothless grin from grandpa. He looked into the sky, only now starting to truly bloom with morning's sunlight, and walked out of the train station. He only needed to find one more page. Ah! The sudden urge to don a deer stalker cap, or, the very least, a top hat, and develop a pipe-smoking habit tingled through his arms and into his fingers. Perhaps a bit of Detective Jack's DNA made it down through the generations to his great-great-grandson after all.

His curiosity pulled him to the handwriting on the journal page.

He's placed another letter for me in our secret spot. I still can't sort out how he leaves them without someone seeing his handiwork. How long did it take him to uncover the loose brick at the base of the chimney? Hours? Days? Longer?

Those details twist my heart into knots. Why couldn't he be like the village boys with their silly taunts and childish flirtations? Those are easy enough to ignore or pacify, but he opened me up to thoughts, to possibilities, challenging me in every way. My mind, my faith, my heart. It's as if I found myself when I found him, but that can't be. I'd never spent much time imagining life outside of my sphere, but his words, spiced with color from other lands and adventures, awakened curiosity and...I don't know what else, but there's a restlessness within me that I must learn to live with or satiate. There is no middle option.

Jane Ridley? Titus skimmed the entry again, diving into this wonderful uncertainty with the vigor of a new story. What had happened here? Surely Jane Cecily knew.

He spent another hour scouring the area without any additional luck. Well, at least he'd uncovered some of the pages. No detective had all the clues on the first attempt.

The bells from St. Michael's chimed with dulcet flair as Bath residents and visitors alike wandered the streets. Titus checked his watch. He only had a half hour to get these pages to Jane and then make it to Sunday morning service.

Tossing thoughts of top hats and pipe smoking aside, he quickened his pace, hailing a taxi to speed the journey. On the five-minute drive to the inn, he reread Jane Ridley's journal entries. No, Miss Ridley's mystery didn't involve his era, but the entire opportunity fed his creativity. After church, he knew exactly what he'd be doing... probably with pen and paper.

MONDAY AND A PURPOSE couldn't get to Jane fast enough.

She placed her chin in her hands and stared out of a massive window from her third-story room, the sandstone buildings of Bath scattered below, spires jutting into the skyline. Loose papers across the large oak desk in front of her pulled for her attention. Per Ethan's instructions, after another intensive tour of the Elliott Elizabeth Inn and a meeting with the management team, she was to begin training his staff on Monday afternoon. Until then, she had nothing to do.

Her gaze traveled back to the window. She *could* explore Bath, but where to start? Nora and Ethan had left hours ago, and she'd made up some excuse to stay behind so they could spend some much-deserved time together without a third wheel.

She touched the edge of Jane Ridley's journal, poised at the far corner of the desk. It would be too difficult to find out anything of the woman's life, even if she was in her great-great grandmother's former city. Who knew if Jane even lived the rest of her life here? There's no historical trace of her after this journal.

She fisted her fingers away from the journal. What if her great-great grandmother's ending wasn't the way Jane imagined? For years, when she'd allow her imagination freedom, she'd dreamed up several conclusions to Jane Ridley's story. All of them ended in great-great grandmother finding love, but what if the truth about Jane Ridley's life only led to the same story as Jane Cecily Warwick's?

The kind of endings people didn't need to learn about. The hopeless sorts.

A rap at the door pulled her to her feet. Titus Stewart peeked at her through the peephole.

"Jane Cecily, are you there?"

She groaned. Why did he keep using her middle name? Oh, the man was a strange one. She opened the door. "May I help you, Titus?"

"Hey, I brought something for you."

She edged back enough for him to enter, and he breezed into the room. His khaki slacks and polo shirt contrasted with yesterday's jeans and crumpled T-shirt. Jane fought noticing how the pale blue color of his shirt brought an almost ethereal quality to his eyes.

"Oh, wow, what a view! Did you see that moon last night, shining down on the city? Wasn't it spectacular? I had to write down a description as soon as I got back to my room from dinner."

Maybe all writers were a little weird. The ones who'd visited Simeon Ridge appeared to alternate between distracted and the forget-to-eat type focused, but yes, she'd noticed the view, the glistening city bathed in moonlight. "Quite the welcome to Bath, wasn't it?"

He snapped his fingers at her. "Exactly. I can just feel something great is going to happen here. Can't you?"

Why did the Energizer Bunny suddenly come to mind? The expectant look on his boyish face begged her to affirm his question. "I'm certain it's a great atmosphere for a writer."

"Oh yeah, I feel like I'm finally starting to uncover the missing link in my stories." He nodded, and an awkward silence filled the room as he studied her, his smile welcoming and relaxed as if he'd known her for months instead of twenty-four hours.

"You had something for me?"

His eyes shot wide. "Oh right!" He patted his jacket pockets in a Columbo move of search-and-rescue. "I tell you what, after church I think we ought to have a chat about this Jane Ridley. I need to know what happened to her."

"Jane Ridley? What do you mean?" How would he know anything about *her* ancestor?

He pulled a notebook from his pocket. "Did she end up with the guy or not?" He unfolded two pieces of paper and placed them in her hand. "It's pretty clear she's conflicted."

She stared down at two of her missing journal sheets. "Where... where did you find these?"

Titus shrugged, a gesture she was beginning to think accompanied his embarrassment or modesty. If she was hard-pressed for an opinion, she'd call the quirk...sweet. "I went back to the station to see if a fresh day would bring some perspective and voilà." He opened his palm toward the papers. "I was able to find two of them in only a couple of hours."

"A couple of hours?" She looked from the papers to the man. It wasn't even ten o'clock in the morning, and he'd already been to the train station and back for *two* hours looking for her papers? She stared at his profile and pulled the pages into her chest. "Why...why would you do that?"

He met her stare for stare, examining her as if coming to some conclusion or other. Oh dear, he was placing her into some fictional world of his, wasn't he? Plotting her death. She cringed. Or worse...a romance.

"It was the least I could do after helping cause all the trouble yesterday." He gestured with his chin toward the papers in her hands. "Besides, a writer hates an unfinished story." His grin turned apologetic. "So, what happens to Jane Ridley and her prince charming?"

Jane switched her attention away from him and walked to the desk. "I don't know."

"You don't know?" He took a few steps toward her. "How...how can you not know?"

She placed the pages into the journal binding. "The journal doesn't say."

"So, what are you going to do about it?" His grin widened, filled with more adventure-seeking possibilities than any Indiana Jones film. "Are you going to look for her house or something?"

"What?"

"Oh, come on. You're in Bath." He waved a dramatic palm toward her. "She was in Bath. Seems like a once-in-a-lifetime opportunity to look up your ancestor."

"Look up my ancestor? It's not like I can scan through a directory and find her address. She lived in the eighteen fifties."

"But buildings in the UK are centuries older than America, and their heritage is protected and appreciated. Little things like...secret hiding spots behind bricks are possibilities to still find here. You have a real-life mystery in your hands, literally, and you don't want to at least try and solve it?"

Jane stared at him, his words nudging open questions she'd tried to coax closed since she'd agreed to come to Bath in the first place. "I'm here for a job, Titus, not some fairytale. I don't have time to sort out what happened to some distant ancestor and her love life."

He stepped closer to her, his forehead crinkled into a half-dozen wrinkles. "But...don't you *want* to?"

His question paused her path to the suite door. She lowered her head, his words pricking at the unanswered questions the journal had unearthed in her for years. Why had she brought the journal? Because, maybe, somehow, she felt connected to this shared-named ancestor and her future fears, and inside craved a tiny piece of possibility in the *what if*. But that's not why she'd come to Bath. "I don't think there's anything to find."

"You have to at least try, don't you?"

She turned and looked at him, drawing curious fire from the light in his eyes. He made the ridiculous idea sound not only possible but necessary. A twinge of pain slivered down the edge of her forehead.

Another chime of church bells from the city below calmed the worry bubble forming in her stomach—or at least distracted it.

"Oh man, it's eleven?" He rushed past her to the door. "I have to get to church."

Not anything close to what she'd expected him to say. "Church?"

He stopped and pushed back a swath of his brown hair, grin at the ready. "Yeah. Steeple, preacher, singing, Jesus."

She crossed her arms and sent him a glare. "I know what church is."

"Want to come?" He rested his palm on the doorknob. "It's a terrific opportunity to hang out with other Christians outside of my usual crew. Gives a person a sense of how big the 'family of God' really is."

Again, this guy left her a little off-kilter. "I've never thought of it that way."

"I love fiction, but being grounded in something real, like my faith, keeps everything else in perspective." He hitched one shoulder. "Most of the time."

She'd never heard anyone speak of faith in such a down-to-earth way. She'd joined Nora's family's church and attended as her schedule allowed, but she'd never grown up with a steady Christian influence. God always seemed to be someone you talked to when you did something wrong or needed help, but as someone to ground you? A base from which everything else took perspective? Well, that just wasn't something she understood.

"If you don't have time this morning, maybe you'd like to join me for evensong at Bath Abbey tonight." He opened the door and buttoned his jacket.

"You're going to church again?"

"I'm a zealot that way." He winked. "Crazy Christian writer. Not exactly a headline- maker."

She almost grinned. "I didn't mean that the way it sounded. It's just I've never met anyone who seemed so eager to go to church."

"Well, I don't usually attend evening services back home, but here in England, evensong services are a special treat. And since Jack is a connoisseur of classic music, it gives me an added chance to step into his mind."

"Jack?" She blinked. Who was he again? "Oh, right, Detective Jack...Monocle?"

"Miracle, and any chance I can take to appreciate Jack's world, I do it." He tugged at his scarf and stepped over the threshold, nodding toward the desk before moving a few paces away. "It's going to be a beautiful day. You ought to explore Bath a little." A few more steps and he looked over his shoulder at her, his eyebrows dancing the mamba. "Maybe it will encourage a little sleuthing of your own."

She closed the door and slid into the nearest chair, a bit dazed in the wake of Titus Stewart, the crazy Christian author. Her lips tipped into an underused smile. He was ridiculous and much too chatty for her peace of mind, but he'd spent hours trying to find her journal papers. And he *wanted* to go to church, even when he was on vacation?

She pressed a palm to her head. Jane Ridley's mystery proved something to pique Jane's curiosity, but maybe Mr. Titus Stewart was an even bigger enigma. She wasn't certain she wanted to sleuth the answer to either one.

CHAPTER 4

Titus Stewart was in her head.

And that terrified her.

Less than half an hour after he left, the walls of her room closed in and she'd found herself walking the pavement toward downtown Bath. People bustled past in their bundled caps and coats, some stopping long enough to gaze into the colorful shops or buy a coffee and pastry from a street vendor. Some shops shone with Christmas lights. Others displayed their best wares to draw in curious patrons. The pulse of the city beat with life and energy and...possibilities.

She passed the Roman Baths, a line to see the historic structure winding from the doorway into a cobblestone courtyard. Jane made a mental reminder to take a tour of the ancient site which brought Bath its name and continued through the building crowd. As she walked around St. Michael's, slowing her pace to take in the gothic-looking edifice rising with spires pointed into the gray sky, the entire building turned her attention heavenward. What a structure! She paused at the bottom of the stone steps leading to an arched red doorway. Did Titus attend this church? Why did it matter so much to him? Her family rarely attended church growing up, unless she visited her aunt and uncle.

One of the church's front doors swung open, releasing a chorus of song trumpeted by a piped organ.

Great is thy faithfulness, morning by morning new mercies I see.
All I have needed, thy hand hath provided.

Faithfulness? Something in her spirit sprung to life at the word, in such contrast to the raw, heart wrenching shame and loneliness of that moment when Emory didn't show up for their wedding. What would it feel like to have someone love her enough to stay, to seek her out, be a true partner? She'd never considered God's faithfulness before. What had Titus said about going to church to see the bigness of the "family of God"? Family and faithfulness? Two things her soul craved to her core.

Over the years, she'd realized her mistake in relationships. She'd been the glue, the one keeping things going. She hadn't been necessary. Faithful? Oh yeah, she knew how to be faithful. But true mutual appreciation? Not so much.

A twinge pricked her conscious and she stared back at the stone and spires. God may be faithful to her, but was she faithful to him? What did faithfulness to him even mean? Titus popped unbidden into her thoughts. He'd gone to church this morning of his own choosing. Had Nora and Ethan joined him?

She tugged her jacket closer around her shoulders and almost sent a prayer into the misty-hued sky. Clouds bumped each other in a scattered array, promising afternoon rain. She peeked into her bag and groaned. How had she forgotten her umbrella?

Quaint alleyways and colorful shops all framed by centuries-old buildings drew her deeper into the city, pulling her from the monotony of her self-imposed safety net of sameness. From honey-coated terraces to open-air markets to museums showcasing everything from glass-blowing to chocolate-making, Bath's unique welcome spun her mind alive. She wanted to see it all.

The first drops of rain turned her footsteps toward the Elliott Elizabeth Inn, but she hadn't made it far when the sky opened. A few steps into the deluge, she slipped beneath a shop awning to wipe her fogged glasses dry. How could she forget an umbrella? She was in England, for goodness sakes. The umbrella was invented here and for good reason. She'd earned her just reward for touring Bath without a plan.

The rain's force doubled as if laughing at her negligence, splattering water onto her jeans and pouring from the awning onto her head. With a squeak, she ducked into the next available doorway. The scent of sweet breads and warm butter welcomed her deeper into the cozy...bookshop? Tea room? Maybe a little of both. Low-lit lights cast a cozy golden hue over mismatched tables and chairs of all shapes and sizes, some decorated with artwork or tucked into corners surrounded by bookshelves. A rich mocha aroma warmed Jane to her toes, and she unfastened her coat, settling in until the rain slowed.

"Escaping the rain, are we?" A young woman, dark hair tied into a ponytail, walked forward.

"Exactly."

"I think you need the last table by the fire." She pointed her pen at Jane and offered a grin. "Follow me."

Jane shuddered against the chill of water dripping down her neck from her soaked hair and smiled at the waitress as she settled into a cushioned chair by the fire.

She shrugged out of her damp coat and scooted her chair a little closer to the fire, the ambiance of the room taking off a little of her annoyance at the rain. A hot tea and one bite of a molten chocolate scone dissolved her remaining umbrella-less frustration. For the first time since leaving Simeon Ridge, she released the tension in her shoulders. Somehow this city, this moment, encouraged a sampling of the celebrated Bath relaxation.

Chocolate certainly didn't hurt either.

She took another long sip of her milky tea, scanning the quaint room from her toasty spot, observing a couple holding hands in one corner, a family of three laughing at another table, an older woman with a book in hand and a man scribbling away on a note... She squinted. Titus?

His slick-damp dark hair lay back from his forehead and an expression more intense than she'd seen in their brief acquaintance crossed his face. If she were completely objective, she'd say he even looked more handsome than usual. Studious. He'd added black-framed glasses like the ones she wore to his overall bookish persona. A good look for a writer.

Hmm...What a strange anomaly he was! Holing away in a little spot like this to write something of imaginary worlds and people. Did he see them in his head? How did that even work?

Titus looked up from the page, their eyes meeting for a half-second before she turned her face away, focusing on the flickering firelight and hoping he hadn't noticed her awkward perusal of his person. After all, the dim lighting cast half shadows over most of the faces in the room. She focused her attention on the fire, but a tingle in the back of her neck confirmed he watched her. A steady heat rose into her cheeks. She didn't want to give him the wrong impression. Just because she thought he looked handsome didn't mean she wanted anything else.

The tingle continued. He kept watching. Her lips twitched from the pinch to bite back her laugh at the awkwardness of it all. Based on their short acquaintance, she could almost envision him fidgeting to join her at the table, maybe even talk about...ah yes, her journal. The tickling in her throat swelled with the heat in her face. She pressed her lips together so tightly her eyes began to water from the effort.

A chair scratched against the hardwood.

Five, four, three, two...

"Aren't you the least bit curious?"

The pent-up chuckle bubbled out and she grinned at him as he took a seat across from her, bracing his elbows on the table.

"About an indecisive ancestor with beautiful penmanship?" She tugged off her glasses to remove residual speckles of water. "I have other things to do here in Bath, Titus."

He didn't respond. Silence saturated the moment until she looked up, his gaze locked on hers and his chin resting on his palms like a little boy waiting for a bedtime story. Who was this guy? Another desire to laugh nearly shook her shoulders as she unfolded her napkin to place on her lap, keeping her attention on her task instead of on those curious eyes. Was he trying to turn *her* into a character in one of his books?

"They're even better than I remembered."

A nervous laugh burst out again. "What?"

"Your eyes." His expression held such awe that she froze in place. "They're perfect."

If he hadn't spoken with such childlike fascination, she might have pondered him as a maniac or stalker, but his innocence paused her retreat. "Th...thank you?"

He blinked back from wherever her eyes had taken him. "I knew they were unique and green, but they're changeful, like glints of light off an emerald. Lydia will be so glad."

She blinked out of the fog of his poetic description. "Lydia?"

He nodded, pulling out a pen and small notebook from his inside jacket pocket. "I've been working on a character sketch for her since church let out, and green for her eye color just wasn't working for me. It's more of a..." He waved his pen in the air and examined her face again. "Chartreuse."

"Chartreuse?"

"No, that's not right. A brilliant green. Emerald is much better." He stared at her again until the silence grew odd. "Yep, definitely."

He relinquished Jane from his gaze and scribbled something else in his notepad, her presence evidently disappearing as whatever muse took control. Why did she feel a strange paradox of disappointment and flattery? Had he...had he liked her eyes? She shook away the thought and smoothed her hands over the napkin in her lap. "And this Lydia is a new character in one of your books?"

He nodded, the top of his dark hair waving back and forth. "The love interest, I think."

Her laugh popped out before she could stop it. "You write romance?"

His grin inched up on one side and that bashful-boy look

emerged. "Not well, if my past books tell you anything, but I'm deter-mined to improve. Jack deserves a good romance after all the rela-tionship mishaps I've put him through. Donna, the disaster, then Lori, the thief, but Clara was the one who broke his heart."

"And what was wrong with her?"

He shrugged. "She was a murderer."

The poor hero! Jane didn't even try to stop her laugh on that one. "Well, if that doesn't kill a relationship I don't know what will."

He caught her pun and joined in with his bass chuckle, spilling an extra bit of warmth into the room. "Definitely. My editor encour-aged me to create a heroine that fit Jack so well she'd stick around for the series. That's what I'm doing over the next few weeks in Bath and a little over Christmas break. Uncovering a heroine."

The phrase voiced in such a simple way pricked at a weak spot in her conscience. A heroine. What would it feel like to be a heroine? "And my eyes are the same as your heroine's?"

"Actually, she looks a lot like you. That's why I'm probably giving you all sorts of weird vibes. I'm studying you because I want to describe her the best I can." He considered her face again then sighed, sitting back in the chair. "You know, it's cosmically wrong not to try to solve a mystery when you have the clues."

"Is it?" She sat back, warming her palms with the teacup between her hands. "Why is my ancestor's story so important to you?"

"I'm a writer." His grin grew. "An unfinished story grates on the very core of who I am."

She swallowed the last bite of her pastry and returned his stare. Okay, so he wasn't exactly what she'd predicted from first impres-sions, but he was still weird and inching into her personal business.

And yet, the annoyance she tried to nurse back to life at his persis-tence failed to flame. "Some stories should be left to the imagination. They end better that way."

He leaned forward, hands clasped in front of him. The firelight played a wild reflection in his pale eyes. Did all authors have some charismatic sparkle in their eyes or just the peculiar ones? "That's what you're afraid of? A sad ending?"

"Real life is filled with enough sad endings. I stick to the happy ones when I have the chance to read."

His gaze took on that dissecting look again, peering deep into her, asking unvoiced questions that tingled her skin. She shifted and took the last sip of her tea, avoiding his face.

"The best stories are worth the risk of finding out the ending, you know? And sometimes, they're just a beginning to the next story."

His voice smoothed over her like the rich tea she'd just finished, encouraging her to relax into whatever magic hum the tea shop and Bath inspired, teasing her to awaken dormant dreams of futures and romances. It had been too long since she'd allowed her thoughts freedom toward kisses and castles and happily-ever-afters.

Wait, what? She snapped the teacup down on the table, as if the concoction fogged her senses. Kisses and castles and happily-ever-afters weren't real life. She shook the Titus-inspired thoughts from her mind, breathing in through her nose and out through her mouth to calm her galloping pulse. "I need to get back to the inn and prepare for my meetings tomorrow." Her gaze drifted to the window while she pushed away from the table. The rain still poured but she had to get away from this tempting ambiance and Mr. Daydreamer's positivity.

"Do you have an umbrella?"

She looked at him as she pulled on her jacket, attempting to keep her face from showing any regret. "I have a hood on my jacket."

He shook his head and drew an umbrella from his computer bag. "Take mine. I equipped myself properly for Bath." He tapped his umbrella against the ground and looked at her as if he'd said something clever. "Persuasion? Captain Wentworth? Bath and its perpetual rain?" She stared back, searching his expectant expression for more clues to what umbrellas had to do with Captain Wentworth from Jane Austen's novel. He sighed and forced the umbrella into her hand. "Never mind. Here."

"Are you sure?"

"Of course. I plan on staying a bit longer to write." He scanned the room. "This place is a perfect atmosphere for imagination." His attention fixed back on her face. "But I would like a favor in return."

She stood taller, bracing herself. "Yes?"

"I think you need a little fun in your life, Jane Cecily. Come with me to evensong."

Her brows skyrocketed and she laughed. Evensong was his idea of fun? Maybe he needed to get out more than her. "I don't know…"

He gestured toward the window. "I'm loaning you my umbrella in *Bath*." One of his brows peaked like a needling dagger to her conscience. "The least you can do is agree to join me for evensong. It's not even a real date if you're going to church, right?"

She pinched her eyes closed to hold back another laugh and shook her head. The man had succeeded in making her laugh more in the last fifteen minutes than she'd laughed in the last fifteen days. "I suppose I should feel relieved that you don't want to take me on a date to church."

His eyes shot to that wide-eyed little boy look again. "Would you have said yes if I'd asked?"

Her mouth dropped open without an answer.

He grinned. "Right. Didn't think so. But the music will be romance enough, Jane Cecily. I guarantee it." His brow tipped. "So, what do you say? A flood-saving umbrella for a non-date evensong?"

She rolled her eyes, chuckled again, and shifted her attention between him, the umbrella, and the rain-soaked window.

"You really don't want to encourage my self-confidence, do you?" He winced but his eyes twinkled once again with a good-natured humor that inspired her smile again.

"Fine." She shook her head. "Evensong for an umbrella."

"And excellent company." He tugged at his collar with a wink. "I'm referring to the priests, of course."

"Of course."

As soon as she slipped into the rainy afternoon, she regretted her choice to leave. Blast the ambiance of a good teashop and a pair of distracting eyes. Her story had been tucked into the untouched recesses of a broken heart for a long time. Was she ready to unearth its tattered and pieced-together remnants for any possibilities...evensong, mysterious ancestors or not?

Detective Miracle would meet Lydia Whitby in a rainstorm.

Titus's smile spread as he typed out the scene, the words flowing with an abandon he hadn't experienced since his first Jack Miracle book. Of course, Jack wouldn't be instantly attracted to her, though her eyes stained his memory, but something in the way she held her mouth captivated him. A sadness to tease Jack's curiosity awake... A different kind of mystery to solve...

Titus sat back and reread his work. Not too bad at all. He sent the sample chapter to his critique partner and fellow author, Jesse Lucas, then shut down his computer for the evening. Time to end the evening with music and the enchantment of Bath at Christmas. He leaned back in the desk chair, hands propped behind his head. A good day's work. Bath was inspiring him more than he'd expected.

He looked out the tall windows of his room, starlight reflecting against the inn's windows into the clear night's sky. November in England brought an early darkness that increased the charm of the city. Golden-hued lights shone against golden-hued buildings like a magical world of fairy dust and sand castles. Hmm... Would Jack think in such colorful language? Probably not, but Titus jotted down the sentiment anyway.

A chime from the tiny clock in the room jingled a warning. He checked his watch. Good grief! With a dash to the bathroom for some mouthwash and a stop by the closet for his shoes, he snatched his jacket off the back of the chair and ran from the room. Luckily, he'd make it to Jane's in enough time to cover for his blunder, but his pulse still rushed as he waited for her in the hallway. I mean, it wasn't a date, but his throat still tightened as if he *was* going on a date with her. As he replayed the coffee shop scene in his head, his shoulders sagged even more. Had he come on too strong? And why did he even make the Captain Wentworth reference? Women thought guys who read Austen were weird, didn't they? Probably. He pushed a hand through his hair and knocked on her door. Stupid. No wonder he could never keep a date.

He knew the turn of the conversation as soon as he saw her hesitant expression. *Gee whiz, he couldn't even keep a non-date.*

"Listen, Titus, evensong sounds nice and all but—"

"I get it, Jane." He shrugged and stepped away. "In fact, I expected you to back out, so if I can just get my umbrella, I'll be out of your way."

She paused in her reach for his umbrella, which leaned against the wall by the door. "You expected me to back out?"

"Sure." He waved a hand toward her. "You're that cautious, second-guessing kind of woman. I get it." The glint of fire in her eyes prodded him further. "New stuff is scary and, even though you don't officially start training staff until tomorrow, it's easier to use that as an excuse than to go with a charming and handsome man to an evening church service on a non-date. Makes sense to me."

"I'm not scared." She shoved the umbrella into his hand.

"Right." He tipped his chin with a shallow nod. "I get it. No worries." He turned and started down the hallway. "I'll know not to make any more deals with you either. Too much for you, I guess."

A sound like a growl came from the doorway. "Fine. I'll come but it's back to the inn right after, okay?"

He spun around and offered his brightest smile. "Great!"

She closed the door behind her, pulling on a long navy rain coat as she approached him. "Why is it so important I go with you anyway?"

"It's important to you too, Jane Cecily. You just don't know it yet."

"Aha, so being a writer also makes you telepathic, does it?"

Riling her was an awful lot of fun. "I have three sisters. I've learned a lot about women from them."

"You have *three* sisters?" She stopped walking and turned to him, her emerald eyes as big as saucers.

"Yep and an older brother, my coworker with the video games." They took the stairs and as she bumped into his side, she cast a scent like the tropical dish soap his mom used. Hmm... He would have taken her for a basic rose-scent kind of gal, but tropical was nice. He probably shouldn't tell her the scent reminded him of dish soap, though. Maybe he could think of something more...writerly? "How about you?"

"Only child." She kept her face forward, her pert little nose tilted up just enough to let him know she refused to say much more. He could play ignorant.

"All the attention for you, then?" He held open the door and waved her forward, her scent drifting close again. Coconut. At least that was part of the fragrance. Hmm...coconut in December? He nodded his approval at the new idea. *Nice.*

"Not exactly."

Whew, hard sell.

"You must have had quite an active imagination as a kid. How did you pass all the time?"

Her lips battled for an expression, but a smile won. He couldn't help but grin.

"I'd read."

He shoved his hands into his pockets and leaned her way. "What types of books did you like to read?"

The battle happened again except with an eye roll. "Fiction."

CHAPTER 5

J ane stared at her computer screen during lunch the next day, a shadow of her reflection peering back at her against the Excel sheet. She'd pulled her hair into a messy bun, as usual. Her sweater matched her pencil skirt, and her button-up blouse kept to the preferred business-style persona she'd cultivated during her years at Simeon Ridge. But something had shifted last night as she sat beside Titus while a men's choir sang some piece about not being afraid...about having someone, God, with her.

She'd been alone her entire childhood. Her mom had worked two jobs to make ends meet and attempt to cover how dirt poor-in-debt Jane's father had left them. Jane became an expert at reinventing clothes into new pieces and siphoning through the clearance rack of the thrift store. She'd learned to pretend, to control, to make things work on her own. Except things didn't always work as she'd wished, and she was often left with a broken heart and no place to turn. She'd never known reliable people, except her brief interactions with her aunt and uncle, until the Simeons came into her life, but even then, as her heart craved to trust in the kindness they showed her, she retreated into herself – the only person she could depend on, right?

As the music had surrounded her inside this grand cathedral, the hymn's lyrics sliced through her cynicism like a beacon in the dark. Titus enjoyed every second, closing his eyes and smiling as if his spirit welcomed the words like a friend.

She'd studied him, drawn to his charisma but also to something else. To whatever freed his smile and lit his eyes with such effortlessness. He'd talked her into stopping for a hot chocolate and croissant after evensong, before they'd made the walk back to the inn in relative silence. He seemed to feel the residual comfort in the music too, a lingering call to contemplate the words, and the experience touched Jane in ways she'd never imagined, evoking questions.

"So, how has your day gone so far?"

She looked up from her computer screen and met Titus's grin as he turned the chair at the table backward and took a seat, leaning his chin on his folded arms that rested on the seat back. "Fine. I have lots to do."

"I'm sure you like that."

She raised a brow. "I do."

He nodded and drew in a deep breath, scanning the room, his brain spinning with questions if their short acquaintance had taught her anything. "So...um...what is the story about this Jane Ridley of yours? I mean, you mentioned a little about her last night but not enough to help me with an ending at all. Did she marry the captain she wrote about in the journal?"

She sighed. Would he never cease asking her about her great-great-grandmother?

He sat up straight. "Listen, this is too fascinating not to want to talk about it." He waved to her half-eaten sandwich. "And you're on lunch break, so you should take a...well...break."

"From you or my work?" She attempted to hold her lips, but they crooked against her will. He really was fun to spar with, and he didn't seem to mind her sarcasm at all. It bounced off his optimism with the ease of rain off an umbrella.

"If you keep flattering me, I may stay around all the time." He squeezed his palms together like a beggar and produced an impressive pout. "Come on, abate this poor writer's curiosity?"

She loosed her chuckle and closed her computer. "I don't know a lot. All I can tell from her journal and a few snippets of information that my aunt uncovered, is that Jane was engaged when she was young, and her fiancé died while at sea."

"The captain?" He scooted closer, encouraging her to continue. He probably got along great with kids.

"No." She skimmed her fingertips over the rim of her laptop, a strange vulnerability fogging over her. She'd shared this story with Nora, but apart from her aunt, she'd never voiced this special secret to anyone else, especially a man. "She met him a few years after her fiancé's death, but, at first, he's below her family's station— at least, her parents perceived him that way."

"This really does sound like a Jane Austen novel."

She squeezed her eyes closed. "That you even know what's in a Jane Austen novel sets you apart as weir..." She caught her word at his teasing brow. "Unique."

He placed a palm to his chest and accepted the label with mock modesty. "Well, that's true."

His grin encouraged her forward.

"She fell in love with him and he asked her to marry him, even join him at sea."

"But she's afraid of the sea, right? And leaving her station?"

She rested her chin on her hand and squinted at him. "You really get into this, don't you?"

"Of course. It's fascinating. Don't you think so?"

She did but it had always been *her* secret, something special and private. Would Titus respect that? Could he?

"I bet she was a little afraid of stepping out into a different life than she'd always known too, huh?"

"I've shared this with you in confidence, okay, Titus?" She pointed her pen at him. "You and me."

"Sure." His palms splayed in defense. "But since it is you and me, what happened? She didn't go with him, did she? And she stayed single until her death?"

For some reason, Jane hoped not, but the journal certainly pointed in that direction. "I don't know."

He nearly shot out of his chair. "You don't know?" He ran a hand through his hair, pointing it in wild directions like the glints in his eyes. "This is like a plot twist of the ages. Does she overcome her fear and race after the man she loves, or does she stay and hold onto this burning passion for him until her death?" He stood and brought his palms together. "Well, we have to find out the answer."

Her brows rose higher. "We?"

"Let's face it, Jane Cecily." He lowered to the chair and leaned it toward the table until it tilted. "You may have the information, but I'm the one with the sleuthing skills. You need me."

She laughed. "I don't even want to know the ending."

He leaned the chair to the ground. "Which proves all the more that you need me." He stood and waved an index finger in her direction. "And I need to know the ending."

"Titus, what I've known has been enough for all these years." But had it really? Every time she'd read the journal, something in her ached for a resolution the pages never gave. Could they even find out the truth? It seemed impossible. "I think we need to leave Jane Ridley to her secrets and—"

"Jane?" Ethan approached from the hallway, straightening his tie as he came. "We have a facilities meeting in a few minutes. Are you ready?"

She glanced at Titus. The determination highlighting his boyish grin sent her stomach into knots. Why was she afraid of this possibility? "Sure, Ethan. I'm ready."

"Titus, how's the writing going?"

"Excellent, Ethan. It seems Bath has exactly what I need for inspiration." Titus grabbed his jacket from the nearby chair and doffed an imaginary hat. "Until we meet again." He wiggled his brows. "And we will because a detective always needs a partner."

Jane watched his retreating back then slid her gaze to Ethan, whose smile spread into a laugh.

"It seems the two of you have hit it off."

"Well, he thinks so." She stood and packed her laptop into her bag, ignoring the urge to laugh at the strange and unpredictable Titus Stewart.

"I know he's a little different, but there's no better friend in the world. Jumps all in, heart, energy, everything." Ethan's gaze rose in the direction Titus had disappeared. "That's been his strength and his weakness."

"A weakness? Exhilaration and ecstatic optimism may be unusual or over-the-top, but a weakness?" She pulled her bag strap up onto her shoulder and followed him out of the room.

"Let's just say Titus has had his fair share of heartbreaks from women who used him for what they wanted and left him to pick up the pieces." He sighed, leading her toward the conference room. "He doesn't know how to do anything but go big. That's who he is."

Jane paused before following Ethan into the room, casting a look over her shoulder toward the inn restaurant. Images of Titus's joy in the music of evensong the night before and his playful enthusiasm and positivity pearled like a contagion over her skepticism. Maybe getting to know Titus Stewart a little better wouldn't be so bad.

Maybe.

So WHAT IF Titus had forgotten to eat breakfast this morning and shower last night? He'd written ten thousand words in two days. Those were rockstar results right there and all because of Jane Warwick. Her personality paired with this wonderful family mystery of hers and ignited inspiration for Jack's latest adventure. After spending the morning researching unsolved mysteries in Bath, he'd come up with a crime as the spine of Jack's newest case. A drowning in the Roman Baths. And Lydia Whitby was coming along just fine. She was hesitant, of course, and doubted Jack's abilities like the best of skeptics, but she'd come around after she recognized Jack's skills and compassion, his charm, and good-nature. That's how it was supposed to be. Good guy gets good girl and they live happily ever after.

At least, that's how it worked in fiction. Real life was a different story, especially in Titus' history. He'd been the best friend to more girls than guys, but rarely the 'boyfriend'.

He rounded the hallway and caught sight of Jane inside a meeting room, her blond hair back in some sort of messy bun and green sweater bringing out the emerald in her eyes behind those glasses. She spoke with such passion, her expressions as animated as when she'd bantered with him in the coffee shop. She often turned to a puzzling board behind her filled with words and charts in various colors, directing the group of people's attentions to different spots. He folded his arms and leaned against the wall, watching.

He'd liked her from the first time he saw her eyes. Well, he thought he liked her and not the fictional person he wanted her to portray. Maybe he'd liked Lydia Whitby at first, but now Jane Warwick was beginning to grow on him. His older sister, though, would wag her finger in his face and say, "Titus, you don't need another woman to rescue. Haven't you learned anything from the last three? She'll break that tender heart of yours."

But there was something in Jane's eyes, in the way her laugh burst out almost as if she didn't want anyone to hear it, that tugged on every one of his hero-wanna-be vibes. His gaze shot heavenward. Someday he'd find a woman who appreciated a hero-wanna-be, right?

Jane caught sight of him, paused in her presentation, and raised a brow in question. He waved her back to work, but within a few minutes, the group dispersed for a break. He pulled her to the side as soon as she exited the room.

"The meeting looks like it's going well."

She blinked at him, her brow furrowed and eyes uncertain once again. "Yes. It is."

"Super." He paused, scanning her outfit. "That's a great color on you, by the way. You know, if you ever want to purchase one of those little cocktail dresses for a party, you ought to get it in green." He whistled low. "Stunner."

Her bottom lip unhinged and a blush rose into her cheeks. Wow, she looked even prettier.

"Well, it doesn't have to be a cocktail dress. Just a cute blouse or something modern and comfortable. You know, when you're not dressed for work." He waved a hand over her ensemble, recalling the forced shopping experiences with his sisters.

Her eyes widened. He must have said something wrong.

"Of course, if this is relaxed for you, then that's...well...fine. Not something to watch football or *The Lord of the Rings* in, but I'm sure you could make it work."

She released a long sigh and pinched her eyes closed, her lips twitching. "Titus, did you really stop by to talk about my fashion choices?"

He cleared his throat and stuffed his hands in his pockets. "Well, no. Actually, I was wondering if you know what Jane Ridley's parents' names were."

Her palms shot to her hips and her eyes narrowed to slits. "Titus Stewart, what have you done?"

Whew, she used his full name. That couldn't be good. He stepped back, palms raised, and feet poised for retreat. "Nothing. Just curious. The more information one has about an ancestor, the easier it is to find out if they lived near here."

She studied him. "How near here?"

"Well, three Ridley families lived in the Royal Crescent in the mid-eighteen hundreds, and one had a residence in the circus."

Her hand went to her forehead then she peered up at him. "The circus?"

"Yeah, but only one Ridley. If I can get into the historical society tomorrow, I bet I can find some other Ridleys in the area, but a name would help a lot. There are a whole lot of Ridleys buried around here."

"What?" The word burst out on a laugh. "You're crazy."

He grinned at the way her eyes lit. "You wouldn't be wrong." He tagged on a one-shoulder shrug. "Besides, you know you need this too. The resolution of how the romance really ended between Jane and her captain."

"Titus, I...appreciate your enthusiasm, but this isn't your story to uncover."

"Right. You should come with me, and I'll be your Watson."

Her brow crinkled. "My what?"

"Your Watson." He didn't wait for her to back out. "I'll pick you up at your room tomorrow morning. You don't have meetings until noon, so we can get a little research done first."

"I have a personnel spreadsheet to make, and I have to take another tour of the inn to make a list of how inventory needs to be restructured for best efficiency—"

"Great! I'll see you at..." He looked up at the ceiling instead of her doubtful expression. "Nine o'clock?"

She sighed. "Why does this matter to you? Why should it matter to me? It's someone else's story that happened a long time ago."

"Sure." He nodded. "But the great part of it is, she's a part of *your* story—where you're from. The past influences the future whether we want to see it or not, but a lot of times we can learn from those stories while living our own." He stepped closer, watching the way those expressive eyes battled against his words. "And I think it does matter to you."

"Break's over, people," Ethan called from inside the room.

"That's my cue." He doffed his imaginary cap again, feeling very Detective Jack, indeed. "See you in the morning."

"Mysteries aren't romances, Titus."

He turned, walking backward in retreat. "Nothing wrong with adding some romance into mysteries, especially for a swell guy like Jack. Like I said before, he's had a rough history with women, but things are starting to change."

She stepped toward him, narrowing the gap his distance had made. "So, you write historical fiction about a detective and his romance life?"

"The crime is the focus of each story, but love and faith are certainly in there too."

"Wait." She raised a palm and tilted her head, the skeptical slant to her lips a challenging tease. "You write about faith in your novels too?"

"Faith in fiction isn't uncommon. C.S. Lewis, Dorothy Sayers, Jane Austen, the Brontes. I'm a Christian. It's my worldview, so it's going to come out in my writing."

Her arms crossed over her chest. "Christian historical fiction with romance?"

He pointed his index finger in the direction of her scowl. "I can tell from the curl in your lips that you have doubts. Which part don't you like? The Christian part or the romance part?"

"Jane?"

The silence between them broke and Jane stepped back.

"Saved by the Ethan?" Titus gestured toward the doorway with his chin. "No worries, tomorrow morning we can pick this conversation up right where we left off. Because I'm really curious about your answer."

CHAPTER 6

"Ethan says the trainings are going great." Nora walked into Jane's room, hair still up in a towel from her morning shower and face as pretty without makeup as with. "I knew you'd be a perfect fit for what he needed."

"I've really enjoyed it. You know how much I love to fix things." Jane ran a brush through her blond hair that she'd straightened from its usual wavy mess and began to twist it into a messy bun.

"You should wear your hair down more often." Nora nudged her shoulder then walked to Jane's massive four-poster bed. "And maybe wear something more...relaxed?"

Jane watched in the mirror's reflection as Nora fingered the sensible navy pantsuit Jane had left out on her bed. Not everyone wore carefree quite as well as her best friend, even in her fashion choices. Jane returned her attention to her own reflection and examined herself with a critical eye. With her hair falling around her shoulders, her eyes appeared even larger and more obvious than usual. Too obvious. She turned to Nora. "What are you up to?"

Nora tossed a grin over her shoulder and waltzed to Jane's closet. "The same thing I've thought for years. You don't show off your fun side enough to other people, and it's time you stopped hiding behind a suit and schoolmarm look." She smiled. "Although you look great as a schoolmarm, I still think it's some sort of shield for you, so nobody will get too close, especially some guy."

Jane pinched her eyes closed.

"Because if you wore your hair down and put on something like this"—Nora pulled out a red, cold-shoulder sweater— "with some leggings and your black boots, you'd show off some of your inner sparkle."

"My inner sparkle?"

"You are an amazing person, Jane, and you hide away. You have for years. This is a great opportunity to be brave. Let someone *see* you."

"See me? Brave?" Jane's mouth went dry. Being brave meant risking her heart, offering vulnerability, trusting someone to catch her...losing control. She glanced back at her reflection, her eyes daring her to hope.

"Oh and add one of those long necklaces and a touch of lipstick for this morning in particular."

Jane's attention pulled back to Nora. "This morning?" She crossed her arms, the plot of Nora's little scene-set clearing. "This morning I'm going with Titus into town."

Nora beamed with enough excitement to rival Rapunzel's first day out of the tower. "He wants to help you with your journal, *and* he's a writer, *and* he's a sweet guy. It's a sign."

Jane rolled her eyes and jabbed a blush brush at Nora. "You're desperate if you're going to use the whole superstition talk."

"I love it when you get all giddy. It doesn't occur enough with others, Jane."

"Well, what's the saying? Always leave them wanting more?"

"Ah, your life motto." Nora held up her palm. "No wait, it's probably more like, 'everything must be done decently and in order.'"

"Ha. Ha." She looked back at her reflection and ran a hand through her hair. She, brave? If she'd had a friend who'd hidden her heart away for four years, she'd have shoved her back into the real world a lot sooner than Nora's gentle prodding encouraged Jane to do. And the longer she waited, the more routine became a safety net. "I...I don't know, Nora."

Nora tossed the clothes on the bed and came to her side, pulling up a chair. "Why is this so difficult for you? Believing someone would want you and be attracted to you? You're beautiful, Jane. I think that's why Titus has that weird habit of calling you Jane Cecily. So, your name will match the beauty of who he sees."

"That's ridiculous."

"No, it's not. You'd fight against my negativity too, if this was me, so I'm not going to let you hide anymore. Titus likes you. Why can't you see that?"

"It shouldn't be hard. I know." Jane stood and opened her palms to the air, turning to face her friend. "But it is. And it's only gotten harder with every opportunity I've refused to take. In Asheville, it's easy to hide at Simeon Ridge, but I...I can't hide here. Even if I tried, Titus wouldn't let me." She nodded, looking down at her palms as if they held some answer to her dilemma.

"Here's the truth of it, Jane. Someday you're going to look back on your life and wish you'd taken a chance. The only way to become braver is to step out into what you fear."

Jane raised her gaze to Nora's, absorbing some of the hope, embracing the challenge.

"There's a guy out there who wants you to be a part of his life. It may be Titus or it may be someone else. You're not going to know unless you try. From all Ethan's said about Titus, despite his"—Nora waved her hands, searching for the right words—"writerly oddness sometimes, I think he'll be the type of guy who wants to see you for you." She tapped the journal. "True hearted, maybe even like your captain here."

The captain, whoever he was, had held Jane's fascination since the first time she read the journal. He'd pursued her great-great grandmother, written her letters upon letters, believed that she was strong enough to join in his arduous life upon the sea. Quotes demonstrating the captain's faith in and deep admiration of Jane Ridley filled her journal.

Nora's grin turned lethal. "And sure, appearance isn't what wins a heart." She waved toward the clothes on the bed. "But a little admiration from a nice guy may remind you that underneath all this work you hide behind, there's an intelligent, beautiful, and, heaven forbid, even funny woman."

Jane fingered the red sweater, biting back her smile. "If I wear the suit, I won't have to change in between going with Titus this morning and training this afternoon."

"Jane Cecily Warwick." Nora locked eyes with her, brows bowing into a V. "Don't even think about it. That red sweater is totally worth it."

TITUS STARED like a dumbstruck teen when Jane pulled open her room door to greet him. A classy red coat that highlighted the gold of her hair hugged her frame. He'd seen her hair down and wavy from the rain, but he never imagined its length reached all the way down her arms to the elbows. "Um... Hi..." For being an author, he was having a really hard time finding his words— or perhaps adequate words. The corner of the book in his hand poked into his palm, and he shoved the book toward Jane. "I thought you may find this interesting."

She looked from him to the book and back, and if his woman-reading skills were right, a sliver of disappointment dawned in her eyes. What had he done wrong? He tried again. "There are at least four cemeteries in Bath with a load of Ridleys, and you can see some of the photos in this book too."

"Of the cemeteries?" She flipped the book open.

"No, of the people. I wondered if maybe we'd actually find a photo of Jane."

Her gaze popped up to his, her lips dropping into an O. Had her lips always looked so pretty? They were pinker today, like Pink Lady apples. A sudden thought about kissing her jumped into his mind and planted itself right in the middle of his good non-date intentions.

"A photo?" She looked back down at the book. "Is that possible?"

"There are paintings of people back centuries and the first photo was invented in the early eighteen hundreds...eighteen twenty-something, I think."

Her brow rose as she examined him.

"I learn random things like that through my research." His gaze roamed over her again as she stared down at the book. "Your hair looks different." Heat scorched his face. Could he be any less suave? "A good different. Not that it doesn't look good all up in that twisty thing or even wavy from the rain, but it's good this way too." And his parents wondered why he was single? Nope. From the long line of blind dates set up by his parents, they already knew why. "Really good."

Instead of cringing, as he'd expected her to do with his bumbling delivery, she pushed her hair back behind her ear and smiled. The glow in that smile fastened into one of his 'favorite things' memories. Something more than her hair seemed different today.

"Thanks, Titus." A blush stole into her cheeks and he looked away to a painting on her wall of a bowl full of apples, but that proved a bad idea because the whole kissing idea popped right back into his head.

He cleared his throat and opened the door. "Are you ready to go? Looks like we have a clear morning for our sleuthing adventure."

"I'm ready, Watson." She chuckled as she walked past, leaving the scent of roses in her wake.

Roses in December? Calling him Watson? A smile to weaken him at the knees?

Yep, he was pretty sure the non-date status needed to change soon.

As they walked from the inn down the hill toward Bath, the morning light haloed the golden buildings below, almost like a spotlight to bring in the day. Titus kept his thoughts to himself though. Experience proved most women looked at him as if he were crazy when he voiced poetic musings.

"There's something about Bath, isn't there?" Jane gestured with her head toward the view. "I love my Blue Ridge Mountains, but that view is...I don't know..."

He tried to tiptoe into the conversation. "Otherworldly? Magical? Almost as if you've stepped into a world that only exists in books." Tiptoe? Nope. More like a jump.

She looked over at him. "Exactly. Like anything's possible."

He nudged her with his shoulder. "Even finding the end of Jane Ridley's story?"

She lifted her chin and nodded. "Even finding the end of Jane Ridley's story."

His gaze held hers for a second too long then he turned back toward the view. "So, Sherlock, did you eat breakfast this morning? We could stop for some go-juice and look through that book before we start truly investigating."

Her grin slanted in his direction, and his mind spun toward Pink Lady apples and kissing again. "Yes, I could use some...go-juice."

They settled into Mocha & Musings, the same coffee shop Titus had called his writing nook since arriving in Bath. The waitress even escorted him to his usual table framed by classic-laden bookshelves at the back corner of the shop.

As Jane unbuttoned her coat, Titus carefully slid it from her shoulders and hooked it on a coat rack nearby, followed by his own jacket.

"Thank you," she whispered in a voice so quiet he barely heard the words.

"You're welcome." He took his seat across from Jane, her head bent low over the book, and noticed them—her shoulders. She wore one of those shirts with the holes in the shoulders. What did his sister call them? Frozen sleeves? No, that didn't sound right. Hide-and-seek shirts? Whatever they were, his gaze zoomed in on the skin peeking through. Good grief! Freckles dotted her shoulders as if the sun couldn't get enough of touching her skin.

His throat scorched dry and he forced his attention to her face.

"Anthony and Louisa," Jane said, looking up from the book as she flipped through the pages.

His brows shot high. "Your parents?"

She chuckled. "No. You asked me yesterday for Jane Ridley's parents' names. Anthony and Louisa Ridley. He was a well-respected mercantile owner in town."

"That's a great start, Sherlock. Now we know who we're looking for in those cemeteries." He nodded his thanks to the waitress as she placed his hot tea and Jane's coffee on the table. His grin inched a little in expectation. "And what about the other question?"

She paused her cup to her apple-ly lips. "Other question?"

"Which don't you like? Historical or Christian?"

"Come on, we've had a good start to our morning, and I don't want to hurt your feelings with my opinion."

He leaned into the chair and crossed his arms. "Okay, now you *have* to tell me." His brows gave a playful wiggle. "And my feelings aren't easily hurt. I have edits that would make Agatha Christie weep."

Her crinkled nose displayed pure skepticism.

"Seriously. I want to know."

Jane took another sip then sighed. "Fine. Number one, the only Christian fiction I've ever read was predictable, preachy, and so positively plain in its premise."

He wrapped his palms around his tea cup and leaned forward. "I like your use of alliteration."

His comment shook her smile loose again, and she stared at him in silence for a moment, her eyes glittering with life. "You're incorrigible, aren't you?"

"I can't afford to be easily offended. I design computer games, so I have a somewhat animated outlook on the world, which helps with my positivity, even if it doesn't really encourage my maturity." Her smile flashed again as she took another sip of her coffee. Yep, this non-date idea was becoming better and better. "And I've been writing novels for seven years. If editing doesn't toughen you up to criticism, readers' reviews certainly will. Everyone has an opinion, and given enough anonymity, they're more than willing to express themselves."

She winced and ran a finger over the rim of her cup. "I'm more of a classics person, anyway, and don't get me started on romance novels in general. Lips going here, hands going there. The story loses its sheen when characters are in such a hurry to get into bed, they don't even know anything about each other."

He grimaced. "What kind of books have you been reading?" He took another drink of tea as the waitress delivered their pastries. "I have a list of books that would challenge your theories of Christian fiction, but I also think there's nothing wrong with making fiction realistic. *I* don't write realistic fiction. I mean, Detective Jack is my dream guy, so he's pretty perfect, but I like reading books that relate to my own struggles and how people overcome them with their faith."

"I've never heard of faith-based books like that before. The ones I read had faith tagged on at the end."

"What if I could give you one of those books from my list? Would you be willing to try one more?"

Her brow tipped. "How about a wager, Watson? If you can find out something more about Jane Ridley, I'll read whatever book you want me to."

He smacked his hand on the table. "Deal." He tugged the book away from her and peeled back the pages to the index. Within a few seconds, he turned the book around to Jane, finger in position. "Anthony and Louisa Ridley." He winked. "The graveyard at St. James."

She peered down at the book then looked up with wide eyes. "Excellent, my dear Watson. The game is afoot."

Yep, she jumped right out of the non-date category with one comment and moved directly to happily-ever-after status. He just had to convince her that this fiction-loving Watson really needed her organized Sherlock...with a little romance sprinkled in.

Nestled beneath a large weeping willow, cradled between roots and over a century of padded earth, two crescent tombstones stood as reminders of two lives. Jane bent low to run her fingers over the wording etched deep into the stones.

Louisa Ridley, 1819-1864, beloved wife and mother.

Years of seeing the name scrawled in Jane Ridley's journal failed to prepare her for the striking discovery that Louisa Ridley had been a real person.

Her head knew the facts, but until today Louisa Ridley had only been a name on paper, like a fictional character. Here marked proof of her existence. A true story.

Like Jane Ridley's.

Her breath caught. Like her own.

She snapped a photo of the gravesite and stood back, allowing the reality to sink in. "I...I can't really describe what I'm feeling right now."

Titus stepped nearer, his face forward in examination of the graves. "For me it was this understanding of how my story fit within a much bigger one. I'm a chapter in the book of my family, I guess."

She turned to him. "Exactly. And somehow, in some crazy way, it makes my life feel...significant."

His attention held her with breath-halting intensity she felt to her toes. "You are significant. God doesn't make mistakes, and He's been working on your story much longer than you have."

She lowered her watery gaze to the stones, following the curves of the etched-letters, counting blades of grass, anything to stall the tears threatening to spill. She mattered to God? Of course, she'd under-stood that truth at a head level from her brief interactions with her aunt and uncle, but for the first time, the realization sank into her heart, tempering the fear and insecurities with a sweet touch of purpose. "A chapter in God's big story, huh, Watson?"

Warmth enveloped the fingers of her right hand, soft and firm. Titus gave a little squeeze. "By Jove, Sherlock, I think you've got it."

She looked up at him, vision blurred with a sheen of tears. His smile somehow touched all the way to her heart. She cleared her throat and allowed the sweetness...allowed Titus room. "I think I'm ready to solve this mystery, Titus. If you'll help me?"

His grin spread wide, adding a sparkle to those eyes. "Jane Cecily, there's nowhere else I'd rather be."

CHAPTER 7

J ane sat beside Titus in the library, touting another hide-and-seek shirt, this time in green. After holding her hand a few days before at the graveyard, enjoying a conversation that avoided any talk about her family over lunch yesterday, and writing five thousand words in which Lydia joined Jack in solving the mysterious crime spree at the Roman Baths, his errant thoughts were consumed with Pink Lady apples, freckled shoulders, and delightful teases of Sherlock and Watson.

Whatever had changed in Jane Cecily from their first meeting, continued to soften her reserve. Her cynicism and suspicion from their first acquaintance had been replaced by a curiosity and sweetness that left him wanting to sit just a little closer and inspire her smile a little bit more.

Ever since their time at the graveyard—maybe even before, as she'd greeted him with teasing and friendliness at the inn—she'd softened, like the waves in her hair. Did changing a woman's hair modify her personality?

They'd spent about an hour at the library scouring through archives of names. Numerous Ridleys had inhabited Bath, but so far Anthony and Louisa had yet to appear in the records. "Oh, look at this." He pointed to a PDF of a newspaper clipping from 1916. "This guy was tried and found guilty of poisoning his fiancée, Hermione Tipton, even though evidence arose to the contrary."

Jane's gaze shot up from the papers she was researching. "One of the Ridleys poisoned someone?"

"What?" He looked down at his paper then to her, comprehension dawning. "Oh no, the squirrely writing brain took over. Sorry. I just got distracted by this vintage newspaper clipping and the time period fits beautifully for Detective Jack."

Her gaze held his for a minute, glimmering a perfect match to the blouse he was trying really hard not to focus on. Shoulders! Freckles! Too much for good intentions, especially since they were still technically in non-date status. They needed to take another walk outside so she'd put her jacket back on.

"A squirrely writer brain, huh?"

"Yep." He pulled his gaze from hers to the clipping in hand. "I try to keep it contained from nonwriters, but the crazy still sneaks out sometimes. Besides, I thought you could handle a little crazy with the whole Sherlock-Watson talk."

"And engaging in research for a possible real family mystery." She grinned, tilting her head and placing her hand against her cheek, almost like she welcomed the crazy.

His thoughts spiraled into Pink Lady apples again.

"Did I hear the two of you talking about the Ridleys?" A librarian so quintessential that Titus couldn't have written one better if he'd tried, approached them. Silver hair curled to sculpted perfection. Wire-rimmed glasses edged to the tip of her nose. Eyes such a piercing gray Titus scanned the table to ensure he'd treated the beautiful books with the appropriate care.

"Yes, we were talking about the Ridleys, a family from the mid-eighteen hundreds, actually."

The woman pushed her glasses up on her nose, her steely gaze passing between the two of them. "We don't have many young foreigners come to see our archives, but I noticed the two of you were very selective in your historical choices, and I thought I'd give you a bit of help."

"That would be great," Titus added. "Jane is actually a descendant of the Ridley family, and she'd love to know more about them."

The woman's piercing attention fastened on Jane. "Do you know the specific line?"

Jane's fingers pulled the journal resting on the table toward her chest. "Anthony and Louisa Ridley. Residents of Bath, as far as I know."

The woman's brows raised to new heights. "Then you'll want to head to the Bath Historical Society, to be sure. They've uncovered a letter discovered in a home once owned by Ridleys, if I recall correctly."

Jane nearly lost her balance in her haste to stand, her feet tangling in the chair legs that caught on the library's floor. Titus placed a palm to her back, the soft touch of her blouse sending his gaze back to the rebel freckles. He raised his gaze to her wide-eyed one, reordering those apple-tinted thoughts. "Do you think?"

"The captain?"

She bit her bottom lip against her smile, catching the giggle that made him think of summer. "What if it is?"

The glow in her cheeks brought out the sparkle in her eyes. Oh man, she'd be so easy to like—*really* like—but he was pretty sure he wasn't her type, which seemed to be his lot in life. Always the best friend, never the boyfriend. Besides, she probably found attractive the straight-laced, cerebral fellas with eight-syllable-word vocabularies who wore glasses just because they held some sort of brain-level status. Well, Titus had the glasses and could conjure up at least one eight-syllable-word or two if he wanted to. But would that be enough to make her fall for him? "It's...um...uncharacteristically lucky." He grinned. Eight syllables, baby. "So we should definitely check it out. Unless you'd prefer to go...um...individualistically." *Bam.*

Jane's eyes narrowed for the briefest second, one brow inching up. "Don't you want to come? Watson's not going to leave Sherlock to solve this mystery on her own, is he?"

She wanted him along. His chest expanded to Thor proportions as he stood taller. "Nope. Watson's as faithful to Sherlock as Scooby is to Shaggy."

"Now *that's* pretty faithful." Her grin unhinged and she linked an arm through his. "Let's go, Scoobs."

JANE PRESSED her palm into her stomach as they walked up the sidewalk, following the librarian's directions to the historical society. *Don't get your hopes up, Jane.* It's highly unlikely this letter had anything to do with Jane Ridley or her captain. But hope swirled unbidden through her. Just being in Bath, near Jane's story, created an atmosphere of possibilities and hope...well, it seemed to attach itself to Titus's smile like a kid's at Christmas. She'd seen as a child that same glimmer in her aunt's eyes when they'd attended services. Was it faith? The magic of creativity? A little bit of both?

She recalled his pure enjoyment of evensong, how he'd closed his eyes and reveled in not only the music but the short message. Afterward, at the coffeeshop, he'd spoken about his faith with such tenderness and matter-of-factness that she'd been reminded of those summers at her aunt's house when church proved a constant fixture and Jesus took up regular conversations.

Her aunt had made faith real. Like Nora's family and Titus, encouraging a rediscovery of something she'd left behind in the throes of a lonely childhood.

Titus walked in step with her, his palm covering her hand on his arm as if he liked her there...like she belonged. She thought she'd belonged before, though.

"Have you always written books?"

He kept his face forward, but his lips spread with a grin in his profile. "Pretty much. My parents have scraps of stories I wrote—and poorly illustrated—from the time I was old enough to piece sentences together."

"I can't even imagine how to create characters from thin air." She tugged her coat closer around her against the afternoon chill. "And figure out how to turn those imaginary people into stories."

"Well, real people help inspire a lot of ideas." His gaze found hers, holding for a moment before turning to the pavement ahead. "And then real events help patch the parts together, but characters hold it all together. That's why people read Jack and my fantasy series."

"You write fantasy too?"

"The Knights of Corton was my first book series before famous Jack came to life. Dave, my brother, took the story world, and we turned it into a bestselling videogame, which spearheaded the whole business." His pace slowed, almost like he too enjoyed the comradery. "So now I can do both."

"Tell me about this Detective Jack Miracle. Is he popular?"

"In fiction he is—everybody in the whole of Yorkshire loves him. In the past few books, though, he's not been so popular in the *real* world. Like I said before, I haven't been great at creating a believable love interest for him. People praise the mystery and adore Jack. They even appreciate the faith elements, but not the ladies in his life."

"You're putting romance *and* faith into Jack's story? And your editor thinks that will help your book?" Reading faith in books hadn't been too impressive, but add the usually uncomfortable descriptions of romance, aka sex-hunting, and it seemed the book was destined to fail. "Maybe you need a new editor."

Titus rubbed her fingers she had placed against his arm. Her annoyance and the cheapness of romance in fiction dimmed at his wordless, gentle acknowledgment of her emotions, bringing a sting to her vision. She looked ahead and took in a deep breath of cool, wood-smoke scented air. Surely Titus didn't strive to write such shallow romance, did he?

"Actually, my editor is right. Jack's needed the right lady for a long time. He's had a few bad ones, and my readers have made it very clear that he needs a strong partner by his side in the sleuthing. My female readers will love that, and if I write her right, my male readers will appreciate her too, appreciate the team." He squeezed his arm against hers. "A guy is always better with the right girl by his side."

Her smile wavered. "In my experience, faith can come across as preachy and romance as...well, more earthly than heavenly, for sure. Having them in the same book seems like a death knell or an oxymoron."

He paused on the sidewalk and turned to her. "Whoa, there are loads of classics that show faith and romance together. Take Jane Austen's novels, or Tolkien's *Beren and Luthien*. And, of course, the Bronte sisters' *Villette* or *Jane Eyre*. Whew, *Jane Eyre* has some pretty hot romance."

First of all, she couldn't believe he'd read female-celebrated classics like Austen's or Bronte's and second, that he argued their literary value for faith and romance? Who was this guy? Even though his arguments were wrong, his reading record was still impressive. She couldn't name one man she'd met who could even name a Jane Austen or Charlotte Bronte novel, let alone argue any of their classical worth.

She resumed their walk, carefully broaching her argument. "Though I appreciate your intentions, *Jane Eyre* really isn't about romance. It's about a woman's rise to independence and self-understanding."

He stopped again. "Are you kidding me? It may be about Jane's growth and acceptance of herself, but it has a whole lot of romance in it. Lots. And why not?" He turned and tugged her back into the walk, checking the paper in his hands before directing their path to the right. "God created romance. It makes sense that people who write from a Christian worldview would incorporate it into their books and show the God-given beauty of the love between a man and a woman."

"God created romance?"

"Oh look!" He pointed at the paper ahead of them. "It's the historical society." His brows wiggled with excitement and evidently their current conversation evaporated from his thoughts. She stared at him, willing him to realize he'd left her dangling on the edge of an unfinished debate, but he opened the door and smiled at her. "Don't worry, Jane Cecily. We can finish talking about romance once we do some more sleuthing." He winked and hitched a grin that sent a sweet tingle through her. "I have a feeling I'm going to really like talking romance with you."

She opened her mouth to respond, but between the heat scorching her cheeks and the tickle of a laugh in her throat, the only thing that came out was a squeak. As she passed him by, Titus guided her through the library door with gentle pressure on her back, his scent of soap and cinnamon gum teasing her senses. Somehow, the combination suited him. Clean, with an added spicy surprise. She'd dated a few guys and almost married one, all of which took up space in her life, but didn't seem to show these simple touches of care or interest in her. Titus's little gestures pooled with authenticity and old-fashioned gentlemanliness. That was it. Underneath his gamer-writer persona brewed the heart of a gentleman. His mother should be proud.

"May I help you?" A middle-aged lady approached, her dark hair highlighted with silver falling around the shoulders of her cable-stitched red cardigan.

"Good afternoon." Titus stepped forward, offering his hand. "We've heard you've acquired a letter related to the Ridley family, and we'd love to see it."

"American, aren't you? How lovely." She smiled and glanced between the two of them. "And yes, we do have such a letter. Quite a find, I must say, and somewhat intact." Her expression took an apologetic turn. "We close in a few minutes, but I'll give you a chance to view it and then, if you want more time, we open tomorrow at ten o'clock."

"We'll take whatever we can get."

"Excellent. Follow me." The lady weaved around some display cases filled with vintage books, scarves, and a few hats. Posters showcasing various historic facts lined the walls.

Curiosity pinched at Jane's patience. "May I ask where you found the letter?"

The woman peered over her shoulder. "The current owners of a home outside of town found it upon renovations of one of their rooms. You see, no one has really done much to the house in decades, if not a century, so it's a pristine historic opportunity."

Jane's breath pulsed into staccatos. "Would you happen to have that address?"

"Of course. And I can give you the number of the owners. They allow tours of the house as long as visitors call first and schedule an appointment." The woman stopped in front of a display case and gestured with her palm. "I'll gather the information for you while you study the letter, but remember, only a few minutes, please."

Jane stepped close to the display case, Titus at her side, as they both leaned in. It was a single page, faintly yellowed with age, and the beautiful penmanship slanted sharply to the right. Her fingers came up to her mouth to quell the tremble as she read the endearment.

Dearest Jane,

Could it be? As if realizing the gravity of the moment, Titus braided his fingers through hers, bolstering her courage with his presence. She swallowed the gathering lump in her throat and continued reading.

I have only a week left before I set sail for a journey that will keep me from you for too long. Have you reconsidered? Please, Jane, I beg you to search your heart. Three years we've danced around your family's expectations and your own reservations. For three years, I've worked to improve myself and show my worth to the Ridleys, for you, but the sea will not wait any longer and I must go.

I beg you once again, come with me. Be my bride. You have captured my thoughts and heart, and I ask you now to embrace me and my world. How many times have we spoken of fleeing the confines of your family's expectations? Have we not shared a kindred vision as well as kindred affection?

I know I am asking you to leap, to leave everything you've known, but you are not content as a fixture in society. You are a free creature, so here is an offer freely given. I will not harbor ill-will toward you, no matter the outcome. How could I? You believed in me when I was nothing more than a cabin boy with a mind filled with possibilities. Somehow, time tendered your heart to me and Providence turned the tides in my favor, but I never grew too far where your spirit did not reach to find mine.

Let us be parted no longer, my darling. Allow the only distance between us to be a breath or a sigh, but not oceans. I will take care of you with whatever power I possess by the good graces of a loving God.

Yours ever,

Edwin

It *was* him. Too many facts aligned with her journal. "Edwin," Jane whispered.

"It's him?" Titus's voice breathed into her musings.

When she turned from the letter to look at him, a cool rush of air hit her cheeks. Tears? She wiped at her face with her palm and nodded. "I'm certain."

His soft smile held no teasing, no reprimand at her silly behavior. With a gentle hand, he reached for her face, and after the slightest hesitation, pushed a piece of her hair away from her face. His gaze never left hers, capturing hers with fascination and tenderness. For the briefest of breaths, his thumb paused against her skin, but the swift caress moved through her with a tidal wave of feeling.

She'd never had a man look at her like *that*.

"You found your story, Jane Cecily."

She swallowed against her dry throat and smiled. "And now we *have* to uncover the ending, Watson, for Jane and Edwin's sakes."

He grinned and looked down at the letter again, to the coat she held in her hand, and finally to her face. "We make an excellent team. Jack would be proud."

"Would he?"

"I'm certain." His gaze flitted between her shoulder and whatever caught his attention behind her. He'd been doing that the entire day. "You with your knowledge and me with my...um..."

"Creative mind."

"Thank you. But I have one request for sleuthing tomorrow that will greatly enhance my focus."

"And what's that?"

"Would you mind not wearing one of those hide-and-seek shirts again?"

She followed his gaze to her shoulder and back. Hide-and-seek shirts? Oh! "You mean a cold shoulder shirt or...do some people call them peek-a-boo shoulder shirts?"

"I don't know but my detective mind is compromised by peeking at your chilly shoulders. It's not in Jane or Edwin's best interest."

She laughed. "What are you talking about?"

"I have a thing for shoulders." He shrugged helplessly. "And you have freckled shoulders. That's even worse. Or better. I guess it depends on perspective. If you were my girlfriend, freckled shoulders would be great, but since we're in a non-date relationship, they're probably bad because I'm going to have the idea of your freckled shoulders stuck in my head." He released a huge sigh and placed his head in his hands. "Let me get my thoughts back to sleuthing."

His unconventional confession following Edwin's letter removed all her reservations about this crazy man. He was good and kind and a little odd at times but in the best ways. And he was honest, a trait she'd missed with other men.

Without thinking, Jane rocked on tiptoe and kissed his cheek, as if it were the most natural thing in the world. His sudden intake of breath shook her as much as the realization of what she'd done. He looked over at her, his eyes close, his uncertain smile even closer.

"Wh...what was that?"

She didn't move, her attention oddly riveted to that crooked grin. "It was a thank you."

"A thank you?"

"And...and an apology." Her gaze lifted to his. "I misjudged you early on and I was wrong and rude. I'm sorry."

"What were your initial thoughts of me?" He shook his head. "No, never mind. I don't want to know because I really like what your thoughts are now, so I'd rather you keep them in the forefront of your mind."

"I like my thoughts about you now too." Her breath caught. Had she really spoken that out loud? "I mean...they're significantly improved."

He pushed another thread of hair back from her cheek and linked it behind her ear, the caress sending the sweetest trill down her neck and thickening the air around her. "I won't voice the thoughts I have about your shoulders, but the ones I have about *you* are pretty good too."

Her smile broke full with a little chuckle sneaking between her lips. Could this be real? This connection to him? It seemed so easy, so natural. Her past relationships left her exhausted or worried as she tried to plan the dates to ensure they went well. But she hadn't planned for Titus—probably couldn't have planned for Titus, if she were honest with herself—and something about that eased the crinkles of worry from her past.

"Here's the address to the house." The curator's voice broke into their sweet tête-à-tête. Her gaze shifted between the two of them, pursed lips relaxing ever so slightly. "Did you find the letter helpful?"

"Oh yes. I've wondered what his name was for years." Jane took the proffered paper. "And thank you for this."

"My pleasure. I wish I could tell you his surname, but I have no idea. Your best option to locate more about him would be a thorough review of the officer and crew list of ships of the era. I believe the library may have some dated back a few centuries." She grimaced. "And, of course, there's always the internet."

"Thank you so much for your help. I'm certain we'll take you up on your advice because we're determined to solve this mystery."

CHAPTER 8

They'd definitely moved away from the non-date category. Titus might not be a true Sherlock, but the whole hand holding, cheek kissing, and shy smiling certainly hinted toward more modern-day discoveries than the name of Captain Edwin's ship. *Yes, indeed.*

As they walked back to the inn, the evening lights twinkling to life against the fading horizon, Titus gave in to the hope. He liked her a lot—shoulders, smiles, good thoughts, and all. Throw in a mystery or two and that just sealed the deal.

"You know we never finished our conversation about *Jane Eyre*." Jane nudged him as they walked arm-in-arm up the hill. "You were going to convince me that God invented romance."

"And you were highly skeptical." He clicked his tongue, teasing another smile out of her.

"Skeptical but"—she tilted her head and drew in a deep breath —"kind of hoping I'm wrong, so I'd really like to hear what you have to say."

"Doesn't it make sense that if God is the author of the world, he's also the author of romance?"

Doubt peaked her brows and urged him to continue.

"The Bible has lots of examples to support how much God wants people to not only procreate and fill the earth but really *love* each other. I mean, some serious descriptions of it too."

"Like what?"

"Song of Solomon. Jewish kids weren't even allowed to read it until they were older because it was so vivid in its romantic descriptions."

"Song of Solomon? There's a book in the Bible called Song of Solomon?"

He nodded. "You should read the book of Ruth. That's *one* romantic book, right there. Sweet romance between an older guy and a widow."

"Are you serious? There are romance stories in the Bible?" She shook her head. "I just never placed those two topics together. Ever. And God being involved? Neither were a part of my parents' story. God or romance."

Her confession spoke volumes. He rubbed his palm over her hand, which rested against his arm. He had a large, loud, annoying family, but there had never been any doubt of the love shared within it. His parents showed him the beauty of a lifelong romance even though they'd been through a few rocky patches, but they'd shown him the timelessness of how to treat a lady.

"There's this story about Jacob and Rachel." Titus placed his free palm against his chest. "That guy was *smitten*. Worked fourteen years for the woman of his dreams."

"Are you serious? I can't even believe that. What guy would ever love a woman that much?"

He searched her eyes, looking for the wounds she voiced between the lines in her words. "The right one."

An emotional tug-of-war wrestled across her features, digging into his curiosity at her wounds. "I've never heard of a love like that unless it's been in fiction, and usually it was linked to a bedroom scene."

He held the door for her to enter the inn, the warmth of the large, blazing stone fireplaces taking the chill from the evening. She *needed* him. He felt it. Knew it. As if God has sent a direct line from heaven to Titus's overactive imagination. She needed someone to show her a more beautiful way, and he'd certainly volunteer for the job. In fact, he'd always wanted to be a hero. "Really? I guess those books are making love out to be only a feeling."

"Only a feeling?" She pressed the elevator call button and looked up at him, the concept clearly new to her. "It *is* a feeling."

Wow, he took the uniqueness of people's backstories for granted. "Yes, but it's a lot more complicated and amazing than just a feeling. It's a mixture of all we are—in our minds, emotions, and wills. I can make a mental decision that I'm going to choose to love you."

At the ding they stepped into the elevator and reached for the third-floor button. His large hand overlapped her smaller one, and a frisson of heat sparked between them. He stared down at her, watching the rush of pink swell into her cheeks. Yes, he could make that choice. His throat tightened, his body pressed a little closer, and the doors to the elevator clipped closed. "Emotions have a crazy way of following our minds, if we set them with purpose. I've written too many books on unimaginable deadlines not to believe the truth in that statement."

"Well, I haven't met a man like that." Her words eked out in a whisper. The wounds won in her expression, darkening the glimmer in her eyes, dimming the smile. "Most of them have primary sights set on one thing, and it isn't thoughtful conversation...or waiting." She looked down at the elevator buttons, her brow pinched. "Besides, they aren't prone to stick around for relationships."

He brushed a hand against her cheek, and her eyes shimmered with tears. "Somebody really hurt you, didn't he? Your fiancé?" The recognition hollowed his center. "Your dad?"

The elevator doors dinged open. He braided his fingers through hers before tugging her into the hallway and leading her toward her room. Was he strong enough to help her see a different way? A better way? Certainly not without God's help. He sent up a quick prayer for divine direction. Was he the guy to meet the challenge for her?

"I'm not saying a man doesn't think about intimacy with the

woman he cares about. We're kind of hardwired to go there, and God created it to be a good thing." He shrugged, heat rushing from his cheeks to his hairline. He cleared his throat. Okay, so this was a new area of conversation with a woman, date or non-date. "But we're not rabid animals without willpower and thoughtfulness. We want conversations and friendship and cuddles too. We want romance." He groaned, totally bombing the attempt. Did he really say the word 'cuddles' out loud? "I mean, I really want the cuddles part too." Great, he said it twice. Hero-talk, for sure. Not.

She turned from the door to her room, hand paused on the handle. Her eyes measured him while her lips froze in a half smile. "Guys want romance?"

He growled and stepped closer to her. "Oh, Jane, I can't imagine what kinds of jerks you've cared about in the past. Obviously, you hadn't met me yet." She rolled her eyes, but her smile bloomed, encouraging him into the uncomfortable fray. "But men have the same kinds of desires for romance as women. Something that isn't shared enough in novels, by the way. Sure, we want the physical connection, but I can tell you from first-person male experience"—he pointed to his chest— "that I'm more interested in making love with my someday-wife than just having sex with her."

Jane's eyes shot wide enough to wiggle her glasses. Oops, he'd said the S word out loud.

"And they're not the same thing?"

Whew, boy, the wounds carved deep in this one. "Not at all!" He took another step closer, wishing somehow to wipe away her misconceptions with a wave of his hand. "They both may end in the same goal physically, but one only connects two bodies while the other connects two hearts."

Her large eyes rounded even more, glassy and vulnerable, begging him to get a little closer. "I...I've never heard of a love like that."

"Just because you've never heard of it doesn't mean it isn't true." His whisper belied how much he wanted to breach the inches between them and taste her pouty lips, but that would probably negate everything he just preached. And...well, he *did* want more than a kiss. He wanted the future Mrs. Stewart's confidence, friendship, and, sure, her luscious lips too.

Maybe even a freckled shoulder or two.

He shook the visual from his mind and stepped back, but she followed him. In one swift, fluid step, she cupped his face with her palms and drew him back to her, the emerald depths of her eyes asking him to answer her unvoiced request. Well, if she was asking...

As they both moved forward, either from inexperience, especially on his part, or from overexcitement, his good intentions paired with her initiation ended in a solid bang of foreheads. Good grief, he needed a lot more of God's help than he thought—even with proprioception.

"Oh man, Jane. Are you okay?"

She rubbed her forehead and laughed through a wince. "Embarrassed more than hurt, I think."

She didn't look up and he could only imagine her internal self-flailing, especially since she'd made the first move. Well, he would leave her with a much better memory than that. He tilted her head up and pressed a kiss to the red spot on her forehead, the tropical scent pausing his movements.

Her fingers fisted around the front of his jacket, holding him in place.

So far so good but he could do better.

He trailed his lips down to her temple and pressed a kiss there. Her breath quivered like a controlled sob. He looked down into her upturned face, but her eyes were closed, waiting...expecting. She pinched his jacket tighter. *This* was hero-stuff.

He moved the kiss to her cheek and lowered one hand to cover her fisted hold on his jacket. Another little shiver of breath quaked from her lips. Those Pink Lady lips. His thumb trailed her cheek. A kiss couldn't heal all the wounds in her heart, but just like the best fairytales, the *right* kiss was certainly the beginning of something magical. And he was a writer! He definitely believed in magic.

With thoughts of sleeping princesses, dashing heroes, and a

bushel of the most magical apples in the land, he took his first taste of Jane Cecily's lips.

JANE RESTED her head back against the bedrest and closed her eyes, reliving Titus's goodnight kiss for the hundredth time. She'd never been kissed like Titus kissed her. After his beautiful declaration about how men wanted romance like women did, his gentleness paired with his faint scent of soap linked like a crooked finger around her body and drew her toward him... and his insane hope for something as true as the conviction in his voice.

His lips had been tentative more than passionate, careful, almost as if he were waiting for her to cue his next move.

She pushed back a tear and stared at the ceiling. Could a guy really *care* that much? Even with a kiss? Maybe a guy like Titus Stewart could.

Journal pages scattered over her lap as her legs stretched out on the bed. A pictorial book of historical places in Bath lay open by her left knee and her iPad, still bright with words from the Bible app she'd downloaded after Titus's goodnight kiss, rested by her right. Her gaze settled on the words darkening the screen. She'd read through the book of Ruth, a story she never remembered from Sunday School but one that opened her heart to more of her conversation with Titus.

True love.

Not the distorted conglomeration her failed experiences claimed as truth.

She'd even tried to read part of Song of Solomon, but the anatomical analogies created such strange mental pictures she had to stop.

But the story that stuck with her most was Jacob and Rachel, the love and faithfulness of a man so smitten he swallowed the pride of being tricked and worked fourteen years to make Rachel his bride. Unbelievable.

Her gaze flitted to the ceiling. And God loved her more than that?

Faded scenes from her childhood filtered through her mind like an old movie and brought with them memories of a time when God had been a beautiful reminder of simpler times and sweeter loves.

"Could you still love me even though I've forgotten you?"

Something in her spirit sprung to life with a beautiful assurance. It was time to remember.

She began stacking the papers from the journal and readying for bed when her attention dropped to one of the handwritten sheets. Jane Ridley only referred to her fiancé as the captain in the journals, but now that his name was known, the moniker seemed to pop from the pages with a life of its own.

There is only a week left before the captain leaves, and I must decide my future—to be separated from my own heart forever or to risk the same fate my brother knew five years ago. Fear seizes me with an almost uncontrollable fury, yet what fate would I survive alone without my captain? Is his strength enough to release me from the hold of fear and the expectations of my family? God's strength is enough for my fear, I must believe, and, if I sever this life I've always known, I must shore up my courage and leap. Oh, what will this letter offer? How will his newest words pierce my heart and encourage me? My parents still have not found the captain's secret place for letters. My captain's sweetest notes have evaded my parents' discovery by the chimney outside in the back garden. He even marked the brick with a C to tease me about his love for the sea and his assurance that I will come to adore it as well. He calls me beyond myself, beyond my simple life. How I love him. If two hearts were ever designed by God to beat as one, I feel his and mine were the two.

Jane reread the last few sentences, stopping on the information about the hiding place of the letters. Could it possibly still exist? She tried to bite back her smile, but it unhinged against her will. That would be further proof of the story.

She hugged the journal close to her and raised her smile to heaven. God was enough for her fear? Her eyes fluttered closed and her thoughts whispered a prayer. *Help me to trust you even with my fears...even with my heart...*

CHAPTER 9

They'd spent a couple of hours Thursday and Friday mornings navigating the local library's archives for records of ships from the eighteen hundreds, but Jane's afternoon trainings brought their sleuthing to an end without any more information as to who Captain Edwin was. The owners of Ridley Cottage couldn't set up an appointment for them to tour the house until Monday, which put the possible solving of Jane Ridley's mystery to just three days. She'd plunged into solving this mystery with the hope of finally discovering the truth, but now? She kept running into dead ends.

Jane's plane for North Carolina left Thursday so Jane and Nora could make it back in time for the annual Christmas festivities at Simeon Ridge. The Inn closed its doors for two weeks to allow all of Nora's extended family ample time to celebrate the holidays in grand style. For four years, Jane had experienced the festivities as the outsider she was, watching and wondering if her future held something as chaotic and wonderful.

A family and Christmas laughter of her own.

With the library closed over the weekend, Jane finalized some of the staff training and supervised the creation of three work stations—one per floor of the inn—where the staff would have easy access to items such as linens, shampoos, and soap refills. Between her supervision and training skills as well as technical aptitude—she'd almost finished the database for staff as well as a schedule and hierarchy for ordering supplies—Ethan praised her work almost daily. He'd already asked if she'd be willing to train his staff when he opened his next Elliott Elizabeth Inn—one located in Yorkshire with a Bronte theme. She grinned. Nora's sister, Gwinn, would be over the moon about a chance to celebrate the Brontes, but Jane? Well, the opportunity to help Ethan with his growing business certainly highlighted her strengths and...didn't Titus say something about a family estate in northern England?

Her thoughts turned to Titus, who sat next to her during the evensong service at St. Michael's, his face uplifted and eyes closed as he'd done last week. Strains of a children's choir reverberated off the arched-stone ceiling and surrounded them with an ethereal beauty, fitting for the Victorian edifice.

Be thou my vision, oh Lord of my heart.

What would her vision look like if seen through God's eyes? Surely, she wouldn't be afraid. She'd boldly step into tomorrow because God already knew tomorrow, and maybe...he had big family gatherings and happily-ever-afters in mind for her too?

The concept sank deeper. What an amazing way to live. Was it even possible? Did Titus feel that way? And how did one gain vision from God? It would take a great deal of trust to believe he held all her fears for all her tomorrows.

Titus's eyes opened, and he grinned at her, sending heat shooting into her cheeks. The happily-ever-after idea came much easier with Titus nearby. She rubbed her palms together and forced her attention back to the choir. In fact, Titus made lots of things easier than she'd experienced in her previous relationships.

His gentleness and humor melted away some of her reticence. Even his quirks made their interactions more relaxed because he wasn't too often offended by her directness or awkwardness. He wore authentic in a quirky prince charming sort-of-way that put her skittish heart at ease.

The music drew to a close followed by a benediction.

He took her hand with the ease of familiarity, as if he'd taken her hand for months instead of a few days.

"I think we should get some ice cream."

She blinked up at him. "Ice cream? It's barely thirty degrees outside."

His grin twitched. "Well, then we're sure it won't melt any time soon, right?" He steered their steps toward Bath's town central. "Besides, it's fun to do the unexpected every so often. Hot chocolate in December? Totally expected. Double dark-chocolate milkshakes in December?" His notorious wiggled brows commenced. "Unique."

"Well, you certainly meet the definition of that word." She laughed. "Talking to imaginary friends that you eventually write in books, chasing down errant centuries-old journal entries."

"Using real people to inspire fictional ones."

"What?"

His smile brimmed. "Yep, first time I saw you, I knew you were meant for Detective Jack. Well, I knew that the secretary to Lord Archibald Carrington was meant for Jack. She's not *you,* of course, but she's inspired by you."

"You have a character inspired by me?" What a strange combination of scary and endearing.

He hesitated and rubbed the back of his neck with his free hand, a faint hint of pink rising into his cheeks. "Well, I've been trying to find Jack's romantic match for years and...well...you showed up and I knew."

"Knew what?"

"He's been waiting to meet someone like you his whole life."

She stared over at him as he stepped forward to open the door to a small shop with a white awning, its fairy light framing the front like a magical wonderland. Someone like her? Or a fictional someone like her?

"Like me?" She walked past him into the shop, classic Christmas music continuing the theme as they approached the counter.

"Well, at first she just looked like you, but the more I got to know you, the more characteristics of yours she possessed. I mean, she's *not* you. She's the one meant for Jack, but you inspired her creation, and now I know she's his match."

As Titus ordered, a sweet but ridiculous thought came to her. Was *he* Jack? She rolled her eyes. That didn't make any sense! He was Titus. He *wrote* Jack, but just maybe...

They took their milkshakes to a window seat. "So I've inspired your heroine just like your great grandfather inspired the creation of Detective Jack Miracle?"

Titus nodded and pulled out her seat for her, a habit she was beginning to adjust to and appreciate. "Well, I'm pretty sure Jane Cecily is better than Lydia Whitby, and, yes, about my great grandfather. In fact, my parents own his family home. He purchased it with what inheritance he received when his father lost his title and lands during the great aristocratic decline in the 1910s. That's where we're meeting for Christmas next week. We go there every year for Christmas."

"Your parents own his family home?"

"He had a flat in Manchester, but he bought a country home in the Lake District to raise a family." Titus took a sip of his milkshake and hummed his gratitude. "Great shakes here. I had two yesterday."

"You had two milkshakes yesterday?" She nearly spit the drink she'd just taken out. "Why?"

"They make me think of Christmas for some reason." His grin wrapped around the straw as he took another sip and then he shrugged. "Anyway, his wife died giving birth to their second child and he never remarried."

"Because he missed her so much?"

He shook his head. "That would have been really nice, but no. Their marriage had been so bad that he never wanted to marry again."

Jane lowered her glass to the table, searching his face for a semblance of the disappointment she felt at the twist in Detective Jack's tale. "That's awful."

"I know. Who wants to read a story like that, right?"

She stared at him, her smile growing as understanding dawned. Of course. "So you're giving him a happily-ever-after in fiction."

He took another sip of his milkshake and winked. "Everybody needs a happily-ever-after, especially people who've had a rough go of things."

She leaned forward, her grin growing. "I bet you still read fairytales."

His brows shot high as if that were the most ridiculous statement he'd ever heard. "Of course, I do. They're more meaningful the older we get, particularly the endings. Life brings a lot of struggles. From what I know of your past, you're familiar with that. Fairytales not only help us use the imaginations God gave us, but they remind us of the hope we all want to see succeed, the good overcoming evil. Kindness being rewarded. Bravery celebrated. Fiction can be a powerful influence." His hand smacked the table. "Which reminds me, when we get back to the inn, I have something for you."

JANE WAITED for him at her bedroom door as Titus ran to his room. He'd searched every bookstore in Bath until he'd located the gift—an unusual find in English bookstores but not unheard of with its international fame. She stood poised, expectant, her golden hair wavy today, which he took as its natural look. After her freckled shoulders and her smile, Jane's hair was his next favorite feature, wavy or otherwise. It shimmered like sunlight on a rain-touched garden. He grinned. That was a good sentence. He needed to write it down.

"The way you're grinning makes me a little nervous about your little surprise."

"Oh, my grin doesn't have to do with the gift. I was admiring your hair."

Her eyes shot wide and her fingers reached to top the wavy strands. Lucky fingers. "My hair?"

"It's beautiful." He pulled the gift from behind his back, but her expression paused him. She still stood there, staring as if he'd lost his mind. Well, it really wasn't the first time someone had stared at him that way.

"You just say what you think, don't you?"

"To my utter relationship-destruction, I'm afraid." He chuckled and pushed the gift toward her.

"Some things are really nice to hear."

Her whisper pulled his attention back to her face, and those eyes, so wide and full of emotion, stripped him of any more words, good or awkward. Maybe not all of his thoughts were bad to voice aloud. He shifted closer to her, mesmerized by the interlay of green and tenderness in her eyes. She needed to hear beautiful things.

"So, this surprise?"

"Right." He cleared his throat and offered her the rectangular box, wrapped in purple with a little matching bow. "For you."

"This...this is a gift?"

"Excellent deduction, Sherlock."

She rolled her eyes then pinned him with a stare. "Don't you think it's a little early in our...um...friendship for gifts?"

He pushed the box into her hands. "Are you crazy? Gifts are never a bad idea. Especially a prove-my-point gift."

Her brows rose as did the corners of her mouth. "A prove-my-point gift?" She looked down at the box then looked back at him. "What is it?"

"Why would I wrap it if I were going to tell you?"

She huffed and tugged at the paper with such careful deliberation his jaw hurt from the clench in his teeth. Christmas would be excruciating!

The paper finally peeled away, her gaze met his with a brow raised like a question mark. "You bought me a fiction novel written by someone else?"

"Not just any fiction novel." He gestured toward the book. "One of the best. If you want to see Christian romance written well, maybe even life-changing, I challenge you to read this book. Even my sisters, who aren't into historical fiction, rave about this one. I'm not much of a romance novel reader, which is evident in my need to learn how to write it better in my own novels, but I read this one, and it changed the way I saw how much God loved me."

Her eyes narrowed. "A fiction novel can do that?"

"Hey"—his palms rose in defense— "if God can use a talking donkey and a group of disgruntled fishermen, I think he can inspire an author with the right heart and abilities to create a story that will touch people's lives."

Jane's laugh warmed him through.

"Point taken, Watson."

He lingered in her stare until heat rose up his neck, surging to his hairline. "Well, I know we've got a busy day tomorrow, so I'll let you go."

Her hand stopped his turn, the lines around her eyes tight. "Titus, we're both leaving in a few days, back to very different lives in different cities. What is this?" She waved her hand between them.

"This?" He imitated the movement, inspiring her return grin. "What do you think?"

She pulled the book into her chest and looked away. "This place and time is not real life. Things will be very different when we return to our lives back in North Carolina. We don't even live in the same city."

"So maybe we don't push expectations." He hated saying it because he was an all-in kind of guy. Probably imagining her with his family around their Christmas tree singing carols with one of her hide-and-seek shirts wasn't the best idea before bed. "We enjoy each other's company, so let's start with friendship."

She folded her arms across her chest, book tucked close. "And then?"

Did she want more? Less? There was no mistaking the uncertainty in her expression. He needed to be careful of his next wording if he didn't want to scare her away. "And then we figure out things from there. No hard feelings. Besides, you may become too over-whelmed by all the people living in my head to attempt a further rela-tionship with me."

"It certainly keeps things entertaining." Her gaze searched his. Hmm...what was happening behind those eyes? "And you may see that I'm too straight-laced and boring to hold the interest of you and all your imaginary friends."

He leaned close, brushing a thumb down her cheek. "Jane Cecily, I find that difficult to believe. You are already one of the most fasci-nating ladies I've ever met."

She smirked but her gaze held his. "I think that's the mystery-lover talking."

He inched a little closer, her rose scent ensnaring his senses. "The mystery certainly enhances the fascination, but I'm looking forward to getting to know you better. There's an intelligent, beautiful, and funny woman hiding behind those plans and Excel sheets."

Her grin lifted on one side, challenging his words. "And you think you can find her?"

His brows shimmied at her tease and the possibility he'd just been invited farther into her world. "I do like a good mystery." She stood close, unmoving, inviting him forward with that smile of hers. "Actually, I do have an expectation for this." He waved his hand between them.

Her brows rose with caution.

"I was kind of hoping for another one of those awesome good-night kisses."

She bit her smile but was unable to hold those lips in place. His thought detoured to all the ways he'd like to hold her lips in place.

"Is that so?"

"You could just reimburse me in kisses for those milkshakes."

She slid a step closer to him. "Those were some pretty awesome milkshakes."

He slid a strand of her silky hair behind her ear. "Afraid you won't be able to pay?"

She laughed. "You are so much fun."

"Don't try to distract me with flattery." He raised a brow and breathed in more of her tangy-sweet scent, begging her to put him out of his misery. "You're stalling. I'm beginning to think you can't pony up."

She leaned in and wrapped her arms around his waist, tugging him toward her. His internal lion growled a *yes* and *amen*. "I think I can come up with the exact change, even."

She bridged the gap between them, her smile covering his with a welcome warmth that made him want to laugh and linger all at the same time. His fingers found their way into her hair, and her gasp fed his need for a deeper kiss. Maybe he could convince her to change her expectations to the forever kind of way. It seemed a waste of time to go into any relationship near-sighted when he had a far-sighted goal, especially if it involved kissing Jane Cecily on a regular basis.

Her palms slipped up his back, smoothing his shirt against his skin. Milkshakes, a mystery, and kisses from Jane Cecily? Merry early Christmas to him!

He caressed the sides of her face, praying God hadn't brought her into his life to be the heroine for Detective Jack's story, but for his own.

JANE RELEASED her grip on the car door as the Fiat pulled into the driveway of a picturesque English cottage, twining vines growing up one side of the building's stone frame.

"Whew, well, that was fun."

Her glare bounced off his optimism. "Not for the bicyclist you nearly mowed down."

He crossed his arms and puckered a frown for her viewing pleasure. She really shouldn't enjoy bantering with him so much, but he made everything so easy...except keeping her emotional distance. Why on earth had she mentioned *no expectations* last night but then kissed him like she wanted to turn an evensong service into a wedding ceremony? He did all the right things. Said all the right things. She bit back her grin. Well, maybe he didn't always say the right things, even if his words did sometimes set her insides fluttering. And he certainly couldn't drive in England very well, but his heart held the right intentions.

"Listen, Sherlock, the roads in England are the size of sidewalks." He shook his head and turned off the engine. "Next time you're driving."

"I don't have my driver's license for English driving." She tugged her purse onto her shoulder and tossed him a raised brow over her shoulder, watching his eyes light up despite the frown. "How did you learn to drive here anyway?"

He opened his door and matched her stare for stare. "YouTube. You can learn about anything on YouTube."

He hopped out of the car, closing the door on her chuckle. She opened her door. Titus had agreed to her statement with rapid fire last evening, so maybe he didn't want expectations. Maybe these little temporary romances were part of his writing life.

She looked over at him and shook her head. He didn't seem like that sort of guy.

"This place looks like it came right out of a storybook."

She followed his gaze to the cottage and pushed those worries underneath the new discoveries they'd made about Jane and Captain Edwin. Could they possibly learn more today?

He rounded the car and took her hand, interweaving his fingers through hers as they approached the door. "I have a really good feeling about this."

"You have a really good feeling about almost everything." She said it as a tease, but it burrowed deep into her spirit, a spirit she was beginning to feed again after a long, parched desert of neglect.

Lord, please help me know whether I should be brave enough to risk my heart again. And if the answer is yes, make me brave enough.

Two knocks at the door resulted in no answer.

"She said five o'clock, didn't she?" Jane asked as Titus backed up from under the little porch stoop to survey the house again.

"Yeah. A nice little old lady too, from the sound of it." His voice edged with distraction as he backed up a little farther. "You know, this cottage has three chimneys."

"Three chimneys?" She knocked again, and as she waited for their host to answer, his words sank in. Titus's retreating form was almost hidden from view as she turned around. "Titus, what are you doing?"

"Just checking for a *C*." His forced whisper came from the right.

"Maybe we should leave and come back tomorrow."

He walked past her to the left and thumbed behind him. "No *C* on that one."

"Titus!"

Jane turned back to the door and squeezed her eyes closed before knocking one last time.

"I'm just going to look at the last chimney, okay?"

Before she could catch him, he'd disappeared again just as the front door opened. He was not being an obedient Watson.

A tiny woman with a beautiful crown of white hair peered up at Jane through round-rimmed glasses. "May I help you?"

"Mrs. Potter?"

She blinked brown eyes. "Yes."

Jane offered her hand. "I'm Jane Warwick. My friend, Titus Stewart, and I have an appointment to see your cottage today."

The woman blinked again, and realization dawned. She raised a wrinkled hand to her rounded mouth. "Oh my, that's right. The Americans. I'd forgotten." She tapped her forehead with her index finger as if providing the excuse for her absentmindedness. "I've not got things as tidy as I'd like, but come in." She waved forward. "Do come in."

Jane looked behind her, but Titus hadn't returned. Great!

"Let me go fetch the dogs from the back garden then I'll put on a pot of tea." Mrs. Potter tsked as she shuffled through the entry hallway into a large sitting room, complete with a fireplace mantle mentioned from Jane Ridley's journal. Thick oak with leaves and birds carved over the entire piece. The same mantle. *This was Jane's house.*

"Was your friend unable to accompany you?" The woman turned toward the way they'd come as if realizing Titus wasn't with Jane.

"I imagine he'll join us in just a moment." She hoped and fumbled through an excuse as the elderly lady led her into a small breakfast room on the back side of the house. With a glance to the window in passing, Jane stopped, frozen in place.

Across the manicured back lawn of thick grass etched in hedgerows, Titus ran at full-speed, head back, as two corgis nipped at his heels.

Jane rushed to the window just as one of the corgis snagged the bottom of Titus's trousers, and he tripped to the ground. Air burst through her nose as she made a poor attempt to catch her laugh. How was his positive outlook working for him now? She hid another chuckle in her hand.

"Are you well, Miss Warwick?"

The other corgi tugged at Titus's jacket while he tried to swat them both away. Jane tamped down her grin and cast one last look at him before turning to her hostess. "Mrs. Potter, I don't think we'll need to look for my friend Titus."

"Why ever not?" Mrs. Potter pushed her glasses to the bridge of her nose and walked to stand beside Jane.

"Because your corgis were nice enough to find him for us."

CHAPTER 10

Titus had never imagined angels looking like Queen Elizabeth II, but if anyone carried a saintly aura in jolly old England, she'd be the one. The little woman rushed forward in her wellies, green coat flapping around her, as Titus attempted to unlatch the little corgi-gremlins from his clothes.

"Doyle." Her voice held a strength beyond the frailty in her frame. "Holly. Come."

The dogs released their hold on him but not before one of them, quite intentionally Titus was certain, paused to huff right in Titus's face.

"I assure you, Fuzzy, the feeling's mutual," Titus murmured, as the furballs waddled toward their owner and were ushered inside the cottage.

Jane emerged at a run, dropping to his side as he pushed to a sitting position. "Are you okay?" She managed to at least get the words out before she burst into a fit of laughter. "Serves you right for sneaking into someone's backyard."

"I wasn't sneaking. I barely made it three feet into the backyard before it was attack of the Ewoks." He cringed and stood, waving toward the house. "Really, Jane, did I mess up your plans with Mrs. Potter?"

Jane's messy bun bounced as she shook her head. "She actually watched from the window for a full minute before coming to your rescue. We both did. It was quite entertaining."

He dusted off his trousers and shot her a mock glare. "Glad I could provide you entertainment as my life flashed before my eyes."

"By corgis?"

He couldn't hold the frown. "What a headline! 'Death by Corgi Attack.'"

"The next murder mystery for Detective Jack?"

He laughed as she wove her arm through his and guided them toward the house. "I can see that one as a bestseller for sure. *Revenge of the Corgis? A Tale of Two Corgis.*"

"You mean, T-A-I-L, tail?" She squeezed his arm, and he thought he'd snatch another kiss right from that laugh of hers.

"You're talking story. You know the way to my heart."

"I like talking story." She snickered. "I like watching it even more."

"Ha ha. You're hilarious." He nudged her forward as he opened Mrs. Potter's door. "By the way, there was a *C* on one of the bricks of the back chimney." He pointed toward the back window near the door. "There."

She followed his gesture. "Do you think that, you know, it's empty?" She left his side and knelt by the brick, pulling out her phone to take a photo of the marking.

"Jane."

Her fingers smoothed over the stone, tracing the edges, enough that the brick moved. She shot a look over her shoulder and then tugged at the brick.

"Jane," he warned, glancing to the doorway. "She's going to bring those corgis back if you're not careful, and I don't know if I can protect you."

The brick popped free from its spot and she peered behind it, shoulders sagging forward with the answer to her quest. "Nothing's there."

He leaned down next to her and squeezed her hand. "But at least you know it's the right place. This *was* Jane Ridley's house."

She drew in a deep breath and nodded, pulling him to a stand. "That's right. It is. At least we solved some of her story, even if we don't learn how it ended."

"Whoa there, Sherlock. Don't give up just yet. Let's go see what Mrs. Potter knows. Maybe there are still a few clues to uncover."

"IF I RECALL from your phone call, you're a direct descendant of Anthony and Louisa Ridley." Mrs. Potter slid a plate of scones and fruit toward Jane on the little breakfast table before adding a bit of milk to her tea. Her brown eyes peered up through those wire glasses. "The former owners of this house, you know?"

"That's right." Jane attempted to control her breath. "I have one of Jane Ridley's journals."

Mrs. Potter took a sip of her tea. "Jane Ridley? The one from the letter I gave to the historical society?"

"Yes, the very one. I've..." Jane looked to Titus and smiled. "We've been trying to find out what happened to her. The journal comes to an abrupt stop, so we don't know if she follows Captain Edwin's plea or stays"—Jane waved a hand to the room— "here."

"I wish I could give you more information, but my children bought me this house only three years ago with the purpose of living nearby then moving into the house once I can no longer care for myself." She took another sip of her tea. "I only learned about the Ridley family after I found that letter and did a bit of research for myself."

Jane sighed her disappointment and channeled Titus's voice in her head. At least she'd been able to visit the house in which Jane Ridley lived and wrote about in her journal. Mrs. Potter's tour brought the journal to life. The high ceilings with wide, ornate crown molding. A window seat in the library where Jane Ridley would sit and read her beloved novels. The notorious smoking fireplace in the kitchen. They'd entered a few unrenovated room upstairs... one Jane felt for certain was her ancestor's bedroom. From the description in the journal of the slant in the roofline to the view out the windows, Jane could almost feel her great-grandmother's presence.

"Where did you find that letter hidden, Mrs. Potter?" Titus took a third scone as his eyes roved the surroundings. What stories were coming to life as the three of them sat in this cottage that surely had seen so much?

"The letter I gave to the historical society?" Their hostess added another spoonful of sugar to her tea and grinned. "I've gotten a sweet tooth in my old age."

"I'm going to be in deep trouble as I get older then." Titus followed her example with the sugar, dumping another spoonful into his tea, twice.

"That's probably why the corgis wanted a taste of you then, eh? I imagine that was the most excitement my corgis have had in years." She chucked then sobered as if remembering the conversation. "But the letter I gave to the historical society I found in a little box upstairs in the corner room." She gestured toward Jane. "The one you think belonged to your ancestor. I found it there under a floorboard. I'll give you the box it came in too, if you'd like, along with the broken letter. They mean nothing to me."

Jane sat up straight. "The broken letter?"

"When we started work on the outside of the house, one of the bricks was loose. We found a letter there, but it was so old and crinkled that my son was only able to pull it out in pieces. I noticed it was the same handwriting as the letter I turned into the historical society but didn't think they'd want a broken letter, so I kept it in the wooden box I found the first letter in."

Jane lowered her cup to the saucer, her breath coming out in a tight strain of air. "You have a piece of another letter from Edwin upstairs?"

Mrs. Potter nodded her silvery head but made no attempt to leave the table. "I can't recall what it says, but it's in the same hand. I'm certain." She took another bite of a scone and smiled at Titus. "I suspect you won't go trespassing in people's back gardens again any time soon, will you, Mr. Stewart?" She chuckled again and waved the half-eaten scone at him before taking another bite.

Jane exchanged a look with Titus, whose grin brimmed across his entire face. Oh, she knew what he was doing. He was making Mrs. Potter a character in one of his books. She could see it in the mischief sparkling in his eyes. For all his talk about story-loving, he wasn't helping Mrs. Potter stay on task at all about the letters.

"You have that right, Mrs. Potter. It would be a sad fate indeed to be eaten by corgis."

Mrs. Potter's laugh erupted until she had to take off her glasses and wipe at her eyes.

"But I am curious about the fate of Captain Edwin's letter, Mrs. Potter." Titus pushed the scones plate a little closer to the lady. "Do you recall what it said?"

How would the woman remember what it said?

"I can't remember, but I can fetch it for you. Yes, I'll get the letter." She pushed herself up from the table.

Jane looked back at Titus, who winked in her direction. Aha, he'd asked Mrs. Potter a strategic question. Hmm...maybe he needed the nickname Sherlock. She stiffened. Nope, she wasn't giving it up. This particular story was hers. He could be the high profile detective next time. Her smile spread. Yes, next time.

After another fifteen minutes of visiting and the retrieval of the letter and decorative wooden box from Mrs. Potter, Titus and Jane sat in silence in the car. Her fingers smoothed over the box, a strange reverence filling the quiet. With Jane Ridley's cottage before her and another clue to this family mystery in her lap, another moment hinged on uncovering the end of this story, and somehow linked to her own.

"Read it again, Jane."

Would the fifth time help? She unfolded the torn letter with careful fingers. Smudged ink and crinkles crossed the page while certain words appeared illegible. She pulled the page close in the fading light.

I have waited...long. This is my last letter and I must bid you a forever... I leave with Cecily....my love. She and the Almighty will have to be enough for my heart. I hope you find the opportunity and the courage to push beyond your boundaries, Jane. The world beckons you.

Adieu,

Edwin

"She stayed." Jane's chest deflated the same way it had the first time she'd read the letter. "I thought for certain she'd leave with him, but he must have gotten tired of waiting and went off with this Cecily woman."

Titus started the engine and turned out of the driveway. "Or maybe Cecily was his sister and Jane eventually joined him? I mean, it seems a little weird that you'd have the name of your ancestor *and* the woman he ended up with..."

"I know." She studied the letter again, looking for any other clues. "But what else could it be? I mean, Jane Ridley eventually married *someone* because she had descendants, but there's no other record of her anywhere. It's like she disappeared from history except for this journal." Jane refolded the page and placed it back in the box. "Not every story is a happily ever after. I just really wanted this one to be."

"Oh, come on now." Titus steered ahead, glancing at her in his periphery. "This story is still amazing. People will love it because it's *true*, even if it doesn't have the ending we want. Who knows? In reality, her ending may have been even better than Captain Edwin." He tapped the wooden box in her lap. "I mean, it really is like something out of a book. Can you imagine how many people would love to read about this? It's one of those stories that grabs attention and inspires imagination."

She smoothed her fingers over the letter, still unable to believe the paper, the signature, and the words were real. If only they hadn't caused more questions than answers. "I'm not the writer, Titus. You are."

The slightest inclinations of uncertainty inched into her mind. If she'd inspired his character Lydia Whitby, was he only interested in her because of this mystery? She shook the doubt away. No, of course not. He didn't even write in the time period Jane Ridley lived. And this was more of a romance than a crime mystery. Not Titus's thing.

Though he was trying to improve his romance writing. She gave the doubts another shove.

"Maybe you could give her a better ending if you wrote about it? Create the resolution you need."

"Therapeutic writing, huh?" She forced a smile then smoothed her fingers over the carved lid of the box. "I guess, but..." She drew in a breath, her mind reeling. Edwin had been faithful until the end, waiting for Jane for years. What would cause her to reject his stead-fast heart? No one should have to feel the sting of such abandonment and rejection. "It's worth sticking it out for the right person, you know? Worth the risk, the fear. She should have gone with him. I mean, in all her journal entries, it sounded like he really loved her. He'd done the right things. And you don't leave someone like him... waiting at a church without the other partner in the wedding ceremony."

Titus jerked his attention from the road to her.

Her face washed cold. Had she said that out loud? The tears dampening her cheeks would suggest so.

"Hey." He gave her hand a little squeeze before returning his fingers back to the steering wheel. "Your ex-fiancé was a jerk of the worst kind, okay? End of story. The right guy always stays."

She ran a hand over her face and sighed back into the seat, Titus's gentleness pulling confessions from her. "I was so lonely and stupid. I didn't realize I was a means to an end until I was, literally, left at the altar with a roomful of guests and no groom."

The car swerved as Titus murmured something under his breath. "Nope, I think the word jerk isn't strong enough for this guy. Maybe imbecile. I can't use the other ones in my head because I'm in the presence of a lady."

She stared at Titus's profile, a smile and his presence softening the sting her past usually resurfaced. He wasn't like any man she'd ever known. So gentle. Truly sweet.

"Emory was after my cousin who worked in my aunt's flower shop with me. I didn't know they'd been high school sweethearts until after they ran off together. The entire experience strained the relationship between me and my aunt, and, of course, it became the juiciest gossip in town, so...I went into hiding. I saw the listing for the Inn at Simeon Ridge and disappeared."

"I'm sorry, Jane." He slipped his left hand from the steering wheel again to brush a gentle touch over her fingers. "Life would be so much easier if people were exactly as they portrayed themselves to be, wouldn't it? Seems Captain Edwin was that sort of man."

Indeed, it did. *Jane Ridley, why did you let him go?* She wiped at the tears on her face and chuckled. "You are too."

His gaze stayed ahead but he smiled. "The good, the bad, and the crazy, huh?"

"Yeah," she whispered, studying his profile. A man who went beyond her expectations. She closed her eyes and whispered another prayer. Maybe Titus Stewart was worth a change of plans.

"CAPTAIN ELIAS CRAVEN." Titus's voice broke into her concentration for the fifth time. "Oh, that's a fantastic name. I'm going to write it down."

Jane chuckled and turned back to the long list of ships' names in front of her. They'd spent an hour searching through more books at the library for any hint of a Captain Edwin but trying to locate first names among the records took forever. And so far, they hadn't even located a captain whose name sounded anything like Edwin.

"This guy died by accidentally hanging himself in the rigging." Titus cringed then shot her a grin. "Or was it an accident? That would be a great way to make a murder *look* like an accident."

She rolled her eyes and moved to the next page. Titus's shoulder warmed hers as they sat side-by-side at the same table they'd occupied each time they visited the library. They'd become such fixtures over the last week that the head librarian, Mrs. Everly, usually had a pile of books ready for them as soon as they entered the doors.

Despite her help, Captain Edwin and his lady, Cecily, remained as much a mystery as Jane Ridley.

"Bartholmeaus Carlinion Senton?" Titus read the words with precision, the syllables coming out with unnatural emphasis. "What parent would do that to their child?"

"If you ever stop talking, I'll know something is really wrong with you." She caught her laugh in her palm as one of the librarians walked by their table.

"What can I say?" He gave his signature helpless shrug. "I love words. In fact, I've written half of my novel since I've been here, thanks to your wonderful inspiration."

"My inspiration? About Lydia Whitby?"

He nodded, raising a brow. "They just had their first kiss and, let me say, I couldn't have described it as well without your help."

"My..." Her face flamed, and she grinned. "I'm not quite sure how to respond to that."

"You should take it as the ultimate compliment, Jane Cecily, and *any* time you want to give me more story fodder, my lips are at your disposal. You can be my muse."

Her giggle broke out with much more volume than she'd anticipated, and she garnered a few looks from some of the other patrons and a glare from one of the much older librarians. She nudged his shoulder with her own. "I've never been a muse before." Not even close. Ever. "You're going to have to let me read this kissing scene. We may have to reenact it."

"Promises, promises."

Her heart squeezed at the sight of his grin, at the way his smile gentled around the edges when he looked at her. She didn't have to *be* anybody else but herself with Titus. All of what made her her— habits, interests, quirks, fears, and all— was enough for him. She leaned over and pressed her lips to his cheek. He leaned into her touch.

"I think I need to include a few more cheek kisses in this book." He nodded, a poor attempt at focusing on the book in front of him bringing a smile to her face. "Cheek kisses are a great combo of sexy and sweet."

Kind of like him. Thursday loomed three days away. Could they attempt to make something work between them upon their return to North Carolina? She turned back to her book but kept her shoulder pressed into his warmth. He still had a novel to write, and she still had a few last bits of information to complete for the Elliott Elizabeth Inn, but she'd find a way to spend as much time with him as she could to show him she was willing to have expectations. Jane Ridley might be her ancestor, but Jane Cecily wouldn't make the same mistake.

"Jane."

Titus's voice, so serious and deep, pulled her focus to his face. He stared with wide eyes at the book on the table.

"What?"

"Um...I don't think Edwin left Jane Ridley for another woman."

"What do you mean?"

"I think"—he turned the book so she could see it, his finger pointing to a spot on the page— "Cecily is the name of his ship."

Jane followed his direction and, along with hundreds of other ship names listed in old ink, read *The Cecily, 1835-1863*.

CHAPTER 11

"Titus."

Titus rolled over and swatted at his alarm clock, grumbling into his pillow at the interruption of his dream. Jane was there, wearing one of her hide-and-seek shirts and a knockout smile.

"Titus." A pounding sound followed.

He hit the alarm clock again then stared at it through squinted eyes. 7:12 a.m. He forced his eyes open wider. He'd set his alarm for 7:30, so why was it going off early and calling his name?

Another knock sounded. "Are you awake? Your light is on."

Jane!

He shot up and threw his legs over the side, not accounting for how close he was to the edge of the bed. In one thud, he landed on the floor.

"Titus? Are you okay?"

"Yeah, yeah. I'm coming." He looked down at his crumpled clothes and examined the room as he stood up. Lights on. Laptop crooked on the bed. Oh, right, he'd fallen asleep writing again. He pushed a hand through his hair and stumbled into the bathroom.

A crazy-haired and puffy-eyed reflection started at him from the mirror. He scratched his head, trying to figure out what he was supposed to be doing. Showering? Brushing his teeth? No, that wasn't right. But something had gotten him out of bed...

"Titus?"

Jane! Late-night pre-coffee-brain hit hard.

He spun around into the doorframe, slamming his knee, then finally made it to the room door. Jane awaited him, her glorious hair falling around her face and her eyes red-rimmed. Well, that worked better than coffee to bring him full-awake. He grabbed her shoulders.

"Are you okay?"

She nodded, her smile brighter than the one in his dreams. "I stayed up all night." She waved the novel he'd given her at him. "Read the entire thing and you were right. It...it was amazing."

New tears swirled in those emerald depths, and comprehension began to sink through his pre-coffee haze.

"I... I never knew God loved me like that, even though I'd been so distant, so indifferent to him. Like this heroine." She tapped the book again. "It was like the story reached into my raw heart and wrung it with a truth I'd never experienced. With a love I'd never known before." Her bottom lip trembled. "Thank you."

He stared at her for another second, lost by her beauty and the significance of her words, and then he tugged her into his arms. She nestled against his chest as if she'd always belonged by his heart. Aww man, he was such a goner.

"You...you don't understand. I've never felt truly loved before." She sobbed into his shoulder, her tears dampening his shirt. "My dad left my mom as soon as he found out she was pregnant. My mom worked so hard but was never around." She sniffled. "My aunt loved me, but I lost that when Emory and Laney messed up my relationship with her."

The ache in his chest grew with each sentence she spoke, each new confession of her lostness and loneliness. He wrapped her closer and ran a hand over her soft hair, resting his cheek against the top of her head. "I'm sorry for all the hurt you've known, Jane Cecily."

She sighed into him, holding tight, trusting him with her weaknesses. He cradled the faith she had in him. Trust didn't come easily for her. He'd realized that from her first glare at the train depot.

"I've had the benefit of a loving family. Bossy and loud but definitely loving. But even without them, even if, God forbid, they all disappeared, God's love will never let me go. It's the same for you, Jane. Don't be afraid, because he'll never leave you or forsake you. His love is always."

She lifted her face to him. "That was beautiful. Did you write that?"

He crooked his lips and worked up his best New York accent. "That's pure scripture, baby, except the 'his love is always' line."

She chuckled and wiped at her eyes. "Nice. I'll have to look that one up and use it as a screensaver."

"Excellent idea. Keeps your thoughts in the right direction."

Her glowing gaze trailed over his face. "I'm sorry I woke you up."

He grinned. "I was only napping. Fell asleep writing, I think, but I got two more chapters in."

Her brows rose, and her attention focused north of his eyes. "Um, I'm pretty sure you were doing more than napping."

He raised a hand to his hair and felt the Darth Maul peaks in all directions. He took a step back and covered his mouth. "Oh man, I probably have dragon breath too." He tugged at his T-shirt, looking down at its wrinkled form. "And there you were, all snuggled in nice and cozy." His attention shot back to hers. "Did I stink?"

She laughed and wiped at her eyes again. "You were wonderful." Her smile softened. "And very snuggly."

He patted at his hair then meant to prop a palm on the doorframe to appear nonchalant but missed the frame completely and fell against the wall. First failing the stupid New York accent then bombing the suave stance. No use trying.

"What do you say we meet for breakfast before you start your work day? Do you feel up to it?"

"I'd love that."

"I'll meet you in the restaurant in a half hour." He backed toward his door. "I mean, if it's our last full day in Bath together, I don't want your final memories of me to be crazy-hair-bad-breath guy."

"I was thinking more like adorable and sweet guy."

He paused in his escape. "I like that a lot better. Maybe after a shower I can be adorable, sweet, and great smelling too. You know, the sense of smell is stronger for memory." He winked. "And I'd rather you have good memories of me."

She chuckled. "Titus, I'm pretty sure those are the only ones I have."

He had one more day to change Jane Cecily's mind about this whole no-expectations thing. Bath wouldn't be the end. As soon as he flew back to the States, he planned to drive to Asheville and prove to her that the relationship they began in England needed a lifelong sequel.

AFTER A FULL DAY of finalizing staff training and inn organization, Jane had walked to the shops in Bath to find some gift for Titus, and she'd found the perfect one. They'd had dinner with Ethan and Nora, but Titus asked if she'd like to take a final walk down to Bath at night together, so they could enjoy the Christmas lights and each other's company before he left for the Lake District. She pinched her lips with purpose. Today couldn't be the end to this relationship. Not when she'd finally opened her heart again and this time to the right guy. No, she was going to ask him if he wanted to continue their relationship when they both returned home.

She pulled on her coat, closing her eyes to recall the way his arms encircled her this morning. He hadn't been put off by her tears. He'd responded, in true Titus-fashion, with complete acceptance even after she'd woken him from his sleep. No reservations. No grumpiness. Just like she'd read about in the book he'd given her, he embraced her as she was. He was worth the leap.

Maybe they hadn't learned what happened to Jane Ridley in the end, but Jane Warwick could change the course of her future. She *would* take the chance.

And there was no need to wait any longer. She took his gift from the dresser and left her room, almost giddy in this choice, this freedom. God loved her, *and* he'd sent an amazing guy to be an extension of that love in her life? Her eye stung with fresh tears of gratitude. Yes, she was ready.

His door stood ajar and his voice carried out into the hallway.

"Zack, are you serious? You really think it could be a bestseller?"

Zack? Oh, right, his editor. She paused her approach.

"I know. Her story made all of this happen."

Silence. Her story? Jane leaned closer.

"You've got that right! I'll keep using her as long as I can. This story is too good not to milk it for all its worth."

Jane froze. What was he talking about? Using her? Story? She shook her head and pulled the gift into her chest as a barrier from the implication in his words.

"Oh, it was easy. She hadn't suspected a thing. As long as I kept to the character, she fell right into place."

More silence. Had she really been so blind?

"Don't worry. Now that I know what to do to make these books sing, I'll find another willing victim for the next one."

His laugh stabbed into fresh wounds. What else could he mean but her? She stepped further from his door, blinking away tears.

"You're right, Zack. It's been the perfect plot, and I plan to draw this out as long as possible."

Oh no he wouldn't! She stumbled back to her room and closed the door behind her. She'd been used again? Could it be true? But Titus wasn't like Emory. He'd been sweet and gentle, ridiculous even. A chill chased away the warmth of only minutes before. But so had Emory in the beginning, to get what he wanted, but everything had changed.

She'd played the fool to another man, and her heart had become the casualty.

Well, Titus Stewart wasn't getting any more from her. He'd already taken enough.

TITUS SHRUGGED into his coat and whistled "It's Beginning to Look A lot Like Christmas" as he walked down the hall to Jane's door. The Christmas lights shone a little brighter with Zack's encouragement about his latest Detective Jack novel. Lydia Whitby had changed the entire projection and feel of his novels from this point on, and it was a great plan. He grinned. An actual plan! He could envision how her interest in Jack's work would continue to change over time into something more—a partnership then romance. In fact, he'd even tossed the idea around with Zack of making Jack and Lydia a sleuthing dynamic duo.

His editor had liked it.

Boy, oh boy, he couldn't wait to tell Jane, to get her perspective. Maybe Jack and Lydia could even tease each other about the whole Sherlock and Watson thing. He'd run that idea by Jane too, although he seriously doubted she'd give up the title of the famous detective to Jack.

After a knock and a long pause, Jane's door opened enough for him to see her face. She looked up at him, her teary, red-rimmed eyes bringing out the green so much he even felt a sting from them.

"Jane, what's wrong?"

She hesitated then looked away. "I think I overdid it last night staying up to read that book, Titus. I'm sorry to cancel our plans."

He braced his hand against the doorframe and looked into her face, but she avoided eye contact. "I...I just want you to be okay." Something felt off, wrong. He pushed up a grin. "Want me to go get you a milkshake? I hear they have magical qualities, especially around Christmas."

A sound like a whimper came from her throat, and she pinched her eyes closed. "No, thanks. You know, I was thinking this is probably for the best anyway since you leave tomorrow, and I'm gone early Thursday morning."

"What's for the best? You feeling bad?"

She shook her head, her lips pinched into a tight frown. Was she angry about missing sleep? What happened to all those nice, snuggly thoughts? "We knew this thing between us was only going to be temporary. You know"—she shrugged one shoulder and raised her gaze— "kind of like a game that would come to an end this week. I think we just call it quits tonight instead. Makes things easier."

What? He wanted to soak every minute up with her. No, no, Jane Cecily wasn't a repeat of his history too, was she? Nothing deeper than the moment? "But...but we were going to spend the morning together at the library searching for Jane Ridley information like we've done almost every day for the past week. And then...then we were going for milkshakes before I caught the train. If you rest tonight, I don't see why we can't still share some more memories together."

"I'm done, Titus. It was great spending time with you." Her voice rasped, her eyes dulled. "But I need to finalize some things with Ethan tomorrow and finish packing. I really don't think I'll have time to prolong this"—she waved her hand between them— "whatever this was."

He searched her face, read the cool expression, heard the emotionless excuses, but refused to interpret them. "This was the beginning of something real, *our* story. I know we agreed to no expectations, but I want to try and make this work, Jane. It's not like we even live in separate states. We live two hours apart. That's noth—"

"And have two very different lives." She released an exasperated sigh. "It's been really fun and you've been sweet to spend so much time helping me discover Jane Ridley's story, but that's all. A magical few days that I'll look back on with a smile but, like we agreed, no expectations. No hard feelings. Only sweet memories."

Had he imagined the closeness? Was this morning just an emotional response to exhaustion? Had he opened himself up to yet another woman only to have her run once talk of commitment reared its head? "I broke the agreement, Jane. I *want* expectations with you. I was going to invite you to join me with my family for Christmas. I mean, you're already in England anyway. This wasn't temporary to me."

She looked away. "Well, it was to me."

Her sentence slammed him in the gut. "Jane?"

Her gaze flickered back to his. "Good luck with your story, Titus. I'm not a part of it anymore."

He stared at the closed door, blinking away the burn in his eyes. How had he been so wrong? Sure, she'd been reluctant to get to know him at first, *and* he'd kind of forced himself into her life, but hadn't things changed after that? He braced his head with his palms and rocked from the blow. Why was he always the one nursing a broken heart?

"God, couldn't you just send me one lady that will stay? Just one?" He called to the ceiling and marched to his room, tossing the remainder of his things into his half-packed suitcase.

With a few clicks of the computer, he changed his train ticket time and sent Ethan a text for a chat. Titus needed his family, the one small group of people who loved him despite his oddities. Sure, he'd share the single side of the table with his youngest sister, Paige, again, but at least he didn't have false expectations. No, he wasn't a game player. Never had been. He was a soft-hearted idiot.

Good riddance, Bath.

Goodbye, Jane Cecily.

CHAPTER 12

Jane stared at the bedside clock as the second hand clicked away another minute. Her head pounded with the same resounding ache as her heart. She'd cried herself into an unsettled sleep then refused to leave the bed even when light finally peeked through the slits in the curtains.

At least the relationship hadn't progressed to the point where her heart broke. She ignored the contradictory ache in her chest, groaned, and rolled away from the clock. A mess of papers and books spread all over the other side of the king-size bed, evidence of the story Titus hoodwinked.

Even as those thoughts resurfaced, they failed to ring true. Between crying and eating way too many chocolate-covered peanuts, she'd replayed every moment she'd spent with Titus. Sure, he'd said she'd inspired his heroine in Detective Jack's book. He'd written a kissing scene after their first kiss. Heat rose into her cheeks, and she buried her face into the cool satin of the pillow. Titus's searching gaze peered at her in her mind's eye, the wounded look on his face from last night requesting reconsideration of his intentions. Had she hurt him?

If she'd only been a means-to-an-end, would he have cared so much? Sure, helping her with the story could have been part of the act. But researching ships' names and reading old letters? Her grin pierced the pillow. Being attacked by corgis?

She opened her eyes and stared at the pages in front of her. But why would he have invited her to evensong? Or given her the fiction book? Or held her with such tenderness when she'd awakened him yesterday morning?

She pushed back a rebel tear and sat up in bed. The new Bible she'd bought at a local bookshop yesterday lay open before her, tossed haphazardly the night before but looking like a life jacket in her current dilemma. She might be new to realizing God loved her, but if what she'd read were true, he also promised to guide her.

Some strange sounding book name covered the corner of the page. Deuteronomy. She read through a few lines then stopped, breath caught in memory. "I will never leave you, nor will I forsake you. Do not be afraid."

Titus had quoted that verse to her. Would a sneaky, self-promoting jerk share those words? That sweet comfort?

His love is always.

"God, what am I supposed to do here?"

The silence resounded with challenge. *Seek the truth.*

She threw her legs over the end of the bed. She should have confronted him instead of assumed he only cared about himself. Her bare feet slapped against the floor as she stood. Regardless of whether anything beyond friendship ever happened with them, she at least owed him the benefit of the doubt instead of hiding.

Do not be afraid.

Tugging on jeans and a sweatshirt, she slipped her feet into a pair of bedroom slippers, grabbed her door key, and ran out of the room.

Silence came from her first knock. Well, after last night, if her assumptions were wrong, why would he want to talk to her? She'd thrown his tenderness away as if it didn't matter. What had he said?

This was the beginning of something real, our story.

Her heart squeezed in her chest and she knocked harder.

No answer.

Oh, he wouldn't get off a confrontation that easily. Jane marched two doors down and knocked on Ethan's door. He answered the door already outfitted in his usual attire—dress slacks and a well-fitted polo. "Hey, Jane. Everything okay?"

"I'm sorry to bother you so early, Ethan, but Titus isn't answering his door."

Ethan's smile stilled on his face. Jane's hope plummeted. "He didn't tell you?"

She crossed her arms over her chest to steady her gait. "Tell me what?"

Ethan ushered Jane inside and gestured toward one of the chairs by the desk in his room. "He changed his train time so he could get an earlier start to Cambria. I guess after what happened last night, he thought things would be easier if he were gone."

He ran away with a guilty conscience, eh? "For me?"

Ethan's brow crinkled. "For him."

Jane sank down into the chair. "For him?"

Ethan sighed and rubbed his forehead. "He really liked you, Jane, and I think he thought you liked him too, until last night. He took it pretty hard."

"But...but he was using me for my story about Jane Ridley."

"What?"

"I...I overheard his conversation with his editor. He talked about how I saved his story and...and he'd keep using me as long as he could."

Ethan's brows rose. "He actually said that about you?"

She closed her eyes, trying to remember. "He...he never said my name explicitly, but who else could he be talking about? We've been researching my ancestor's story for over a week. I'm the only *she* whose story he's been interested in."

"I'm not too sure about that, Jane." Ethan tapped a few keys on his laptop. "He sent me the first six chapters of his new novel. Without a doubt, this has been his best work, but there's nothing in this story related to a nineteenth-century woman and her mysterious captain."

"But...but I don't understand. He kept mentioning using *her*."

"This may provide some clarity. It's at the beginning of his novel."

Ethan turned his laptop around. A blank white screen blotted by only a few lines shone into the dim room.

To Jane Cecily,
Without you, this romance would have never found its way onto the page and into my heart.
Thank you for being the inspiration I needed.

She read the words then reread them. If the story wasn't about Jane Ridley and the woman mentioned in the phone conversation wasn't Jane Warwick, then who... Her gaze met Ethan's.

"He was talking about Lydia Whitby."

"The heroine?" Ethan's shoulders relaxed. "That would make sense."

"But...he talked about her as if she were a real person."

Ethan chuckled and closed the laptop. "To Titus, sometimes his imaginary friends are real to him."

That's true. When he'd mentioned Jack and Lydia and anyone else in his story world, he spoke about them as if he'd just finished having conversations with them, as if their stories were as alive to him as the one he was living.

"Oh Ethan, I've...I've really hurt him." She squeezed her eyes closed as her words came back to taunt her. *It was temporary to me.* "I've got to get in touch with him."

"Phone reception is tricky where his family's home is." He grinned. "Kind of like your Blue Ridge Mountains, but you could email him. Maybe smooth things over until you two could meet again."

Old fear gnawed against her newfound confidence. What good would it do to email him? His wounded expression flashed back to mind. *It wasn't temporary to me.* She'd ruined any chance with Titus Stewart, hadn't she?

With a sigh, she pushed a hand through her hair and stood.

"Thanks, Ethan, for helping me talk through this and for giving me the opportunity to work in your lovely inn."

"You're made for this, Jane. I can't thank *you* enough, and I have every expectation to bring you over to Yorkshire in about six months to help with the new inn I'm opening there."

She swallowed through the growing lump in her throat and tightened her smile. "Sounds like another great opportunity. I look forward to it."

Her slippered feet took her back to her room, and she dropped to her bed, burying her face in her hands. Why, oh why, had she jumped to conclusions without any hard evidence at all. She groaned and fell back against the billowing comforter. She'd ruined her own love story and wounded a good guy by allowing old insecurities to invent ridiculous assumptions. Titus's proclivity for talking about his imaginary friends hadn't helped, but she couldn't place any of the blame on him. It was all her fault.

Her gaze moved the length of the room and landed on her suitcase. It was time to go back to what she knew, to her safe place.

To where she knew the nice, predictable scenes in her lonely little story.

A place to hide from another mistake, except this time, she'd hurt someone.

JANE PUSHED OPEN the door to the library in Bath. Her bags were packed. Her clothes set out for the next day to travel home. She'd arrived in Bath weeks ago dreaming of returning to the predictability and routine of Simeon Ridge, but now...now she wasn't the same person. Something had changed in her. Not only had she rediscovered her childhood faith, she'd reopened her heart to love.

Ethan thought she should contact Titus and explain, but why would he forgive her? She'd basically thrown his kindness into his face, failing to value him as he'd done to her. Yet she couldn't stand the thought of him being somewhere in the world and thinking ill of her. What if he forgave her? What if he wanted to pursue this relationship? What if God had placed him in her life as one of the keys to her happily ever after and she was letting him leave?

In the end, she stood on the same kind of precipice as Jane Ridley had over one hundred years ago.

Her former life waited like a safety net.

An uncertain future held the promise of something even sweeter but at the risk of breaking her heart and being rejected.

She closed her eyes and breathed in the scent of books and time, praying for clarity. She *wanted* to take the chance on Titus Stewart all the way down to her trembling knees, but oh, how she'd wounded him. He didn't deserve some indecisive, quick-tempered person like her.

"Back again?" The librarian's greeting pulled Jane to the desk. She'd been the same one who'd helped her and Titus locate Edwin's letter, the same one to point them in the direction of the ship's accounts. Her gray eyes glimmered with the curiosity of a woman who'd never grown up completely. Jane admired that. Titus would be that kind of older man.

The kind with a constant twinkle.

She smiled at the thought of him in forty or fifty years, his imagination still lighting his eyes with the wonder of a child's.

Jane placed the book down on the counter. "I'm returning this. Thank you so much for allowing me to borrow it for the time I've been here."

"Leaving, are you?"

"Yes. I head home tomorrow." Jane smoothed her palm over the cover of the book and pushed it toward the librarian.

"And did you and your man ever solve your mystery about the captain and the lady?"

"We discovered the captain's first name and his ship's name, but we never uncovered who he married, if anyone."

"I was considering your dilemma last evening, and I thought of one more place you may wish to look." She raised an index finger in the air like a bookmark to her thoughts. "I happened to locate a detailed list of ships' crew lists from the nineteenth century and thought you'd care to see it."

Jane forced a smile. What did it hurt to take one more look, especially since the sweet librarian went to so much trouble? "I would. Thank you."

The woman turned to the shelf behind her and brought out a thick, hard-bound book with aged pages, the light in her eyes growing with mischief. "*The Cecily*, am I right?"

A sudden rush of awareness stole the volume in her response. "Yes." She swallowed. "*The Cecily*."

The woman held more knowledge in her expression than her small smile portrayed. Without unlinking her gaze from Jane's, she opened the book to a bookmarked spot and turned the pages around, so Jane could read them. With a second's hesitation, Jane broke the link and looked at the pages, starting at the top left. A ship's name was listed followed by a list of the captain and crew. *The Calliope. The Carolina. The Ceanothus.*

Her attention froze on the next words. *The Cecily.*

She fisted her palm against the pale page and held her breath. *Captain Edwin Knight.*

Her grin slipped free. Knight? How ironic but had he really swept his princess away? Her vision blurred as she skimmed the list of crew names. At the very end a simple sentence solved the mystery her heart had been afraid to find.

Also traveling aboard ship was Mrs. Jane Knight, wife to Captain Knight.

She blinked her vision clear and reread the sentence. The answer! Jane Ridley had married the captain. She'd leapt into the unknown. Jane's gaze returned to the librarian, whose smile remained unchanged, but the twinkle in her eyes deepened. "I take it you found what you were looking for?"

Jane nodded, her grin turning into a giggle. She caught the sound with her hand. "Yes. Thank you."

"Very good." The woman looked around the room then back to Jane. "I suppose your Mr. Stewart would enjoy knowing your findings."

Her Mr. Stewart? She took a photo of the page and stepped back from the counter. "He would."

"An ending to your mystery, finally?"

"The ending of Jane Rid...Jane Knight's story. But I think it might be the beginning of *mine*."

"Your Mr. Stewart should hear about this, then. Don't you think?"

"My Mr. Stewart," Jane whispered. She looked up, her smile growing, as she backed away from the desk. "You're right and I think I know exactly where to find him."

PAIGE HUNG from Titus's neck as he raised her up higher to place an ornament on the Christmas tree. Coming home had been the best thing for him. Even if his oldest brother and sister hadn't arrived from the States yet, the younger siblings provided a fantastic buoy to his heartbreak. His two-year-old niece, Brynn, tugged with impressive force at the bottom of his trousers, attempting to get his attention, and his thoughts spun back to corgis. He almost grinned.

"I'm glad to hear you've gotten your writing mojo back, Titus." His younger yet married brother, Devlin, swept Brynn into his arms, and she released a carefree giggle. "Mom said the chapters you sent her are amazing. I can't wait to read them."

"Thanks." He exchanged a look with Mom, the only person who'd heard the whole story about Jane Cecily and his doldrums of disappointment. "I think it's my best work too."

"I heard you've added *romance*." Paige slid from his back, sporting a raised eyebrow like the sassy teenager she was trying to be.

"Too bad it has to be fictional, right, Titus?" His brother's words unintentionally needled the fresh wound.

"Yeah, too bad." He drew in a deep breath and stared up at the half-decorated Christmas tree, almost making a Christmas miracle wish like any faithful Hallmark-movie watcher.

"Titus, I could really use your help with the fairy lights on the back deck." Mom to the rescue. "Would you let Paige, Devlin, and Shima finish up with the tree?"

"Sure thing, Mom."

The doorbell rung through the house.

"Keith, someone's at the door." Mom gestured toward Dad, who was desperately trying to pick up American news on the decidedly British tele. "It's probably Paul and Tina. Could you get it? I know they'll need some help with the kids."

Dad hopped up from his chair and headed for the door.

Titus followed his mom through the kitchen, down the hallway, and out the back-patio door into the crisp December air. In the distance the sun set behind the mountains across Derwentwater, glimmering golden into the lake. His chest ached from the beauty. The wintry night was made for romance, but it looked like he'd be teaming up with Paige again on the family's Christmas trivia game.

Jane would have loved his family.

Their teasing and fun-loving natures might have intimidated her at first, but, she'd have gotten used to them. And, he felt pretty sure she needed them too. He shook his head, trying to force images of her and her Pink Lady smile from his mind.

"You really liked her, didn't you?"

Titus took the string of lights from his mom and began carving the path from the tall holly bush near the large glass door up around the frame. "I thought she liked me too. I mean, I know I've been wrong before, but...but there was something different about her. We matched, somehow."

"Could you have read her intentions wrong, Titus? Maybe she was confused or something? Women aren't known for *always* being right."

He grinned at his mom's gentle humor and then sighed. "She sounded pretty certain."

"Not everyone is as notoriously honest and open as you."

His chuckle arose, reluctantly. "Or as weird. I need a sign on my forehead that reads, 'only the brave and somewhat eccentric need apply'."

"Titus." Mom paused twisting the lights around the matching holly tree and stared through the door into the kitchen. "What did she look like?"

Strange question. He untangled a little light-knot. "Well, she had this massive amount of golden hair and this cute little nose." His words turned into frosted breath on the chilly air, but memories infused his chest with a bittersweet warmth. "And she was the perfect hugging size."

"And did she have remarkable green eyes?"

Titus turned all the way around. "How did you—"

There Jane stood, staring at him from the other side of the patio doors, her remarkable green eyes as round and emerald as ever. He looked over at his mom, whose smile seemed to understand something Titus was afraid to believe.

He set down the fairy lights and pushed open the door, rubbing his eyes to make sure his vision worked. After all, he wasn't wearing his glasses at the moment. "Jane?"

"Hey, Titus." Her words spilled out, rushed. "I'm sorry to show up unannounced, especially during the holidays, but I really needed to talk to you."

Her hair fell in waves around her and freckles peeked from the shoulders of her red blouse. Oh man, she'd pulled out the whole arsenal for this visit. He was a goner all over again. "Don't you have a plane to catch tomorrow morning?"

She hesitated. "I..." She looked down at her fidgeting fingers. "Well, I'm not sure right now if I do or not."

He should understand her implication, but somehow his mind refused to take it in. It seemed way too fictional to believe. Could she mean she wanted to...stay with him and his family? Maybe his imagination *was* taking over, because here Jane Cecily Warwick stood in his family's home at Christmastime, just like he'd hoped...all Christmas-miracle-like and everything.

Mom moved in his periphery, stepping toward where his Dad stood in the kitchen doorway. Titus blinked back to the present, scratching his shocked mind for words. "This...this is my mom, Julie

Stewart." He gestured toward his dad. "And I guess you've already met my dad, Keith."

She smiled at them both. "Yes. Nice to meet you."

"And you. We've heard a lot about you, Jane." Mom's gentle voice entering the surreal situation seemed to ground Titus in reality. He wasn't dreaming.

"It's the first I've heard about a Jane Cecily," Dad announced with a laugh. "But any friend of Titus's is a friend of ours."

Jane's gaze found his, asking if his father's assessment proved true.

"I *thought* we were friends."

"We are." She stepped forward, her gaze holding his. "I mean, I hope we are."

"Keith, I think we should help Devlin and the others decorate the tree." Mom slipped past him and hooked her arm through Dad's as they disappeared from the room.

Titus couldn't stop staring. She should be in Bath preparing to leave on a plane for North Carolina, shouldn't she? Unless...He blinked, an idea rushing to the surface. Unless, she wanted something more than temporary.

"I needed to apologize to you in person." She looked up, gaze probing his before she returned her attention to the ground. "I overheard your conversation to your editor about your story and somehow thought you were referring to using *me* to inspire Jack's novel."

His brows rose. He was still trying to sort out what she was doing in his home and now she brought up his conversation with his editor? Is this what he sounded like to people when he talked about multiple stories at once? "But you did inspire Jack's story. You were the initial inspiration for Lydia Whitby and getting to know you brought *her* to life."

"Yes, right." She waved her hand in the air and pinched her eyes closed. "But when you talked about using 'her'"—she made air quotes with her fingers— "to get as much story out of her as you could. It sounded like you were stealing *my* story for your own purposes."

He squinted, trying to follow along. "I meant Lydia Whitby. Her character has revolutionized my entire plan for the Detective Jack books. In fact, I'm sure Lydia's even going to be surprised by her involvement in the stories. She doesn't have any idea of what's coming, but I have all sorts of things planned." His palms came up in the air. "And I never plan."

She chuckled. "There you go talking about her like she's a real person again." Her smile softened in such a way, he shifted a step closer. The fact she'd traveled all the way to Cambria from Bath had to be a good sign, even for his poor woman-reading skills. Something much more than temporary.

"It's an occupational hazard. I think I warned you about that."

Her smile flickered before she returned her focus to her fidgeting fingers. "You said...you said she doesn't suspect anything, and during the phone call it sounded as if you were taking advantage of me only to get information about Jane Ridley, so I thought that's all I was." Her gaze returned to his. "A tool to help your story."

The one-sided conversations of an author and his editor had the potential to send all sorts of mixed messages. What if she'd overheard one of the murder scene conversations? He cringed.

"I...I know that's not what the conversation was about *now*, and I just needed you to know how sorry I am for what I said to you." Her gaze wavered in his. "For...for hurting you. I...I would never want to hurt you, Titus."

And she'd thought he'd used her like her ex-fiancé? He examined her downturned face, the frown so pink and sad. No wonder she'd pulled away. But if she took the train all the way to Cambria just to clarify a misinterpretation when a phone call could have done the same, there had to be more to her tale. A heart-lot more.

"Well, Jane Cecily, you *do* help my story."

"I know, the whole sleuthing experience inspired you." She cleared her throat and looked everywhere else in the room except at him. "And the kissing scenes." Her eyes fluttered closed again and a beautiful flush of pink rose into her cheeks.

"I wasn't talking about Detective Jack's story."

Her fidgeting stopped, and she looked up at him. "You weren't?"

He edged another step closer, his fingers stuffed into his pockets and twitching for the touch of her hair. "No. I was talking about Titus Stewart's story."

Jane's grin bloomed so brightly he felt the residual glow in his chest. Festive. Christmassy.

"Oh man, that was a great line, bro. You should totally put it in a book."

Paige peeked around the corner of the kitchen, her braces-filled grin in silvery shine and her blue eyes dancing with mischief-making and fairytales.

"Jane Cecily, this is my sister, Paige," he said through gritted teeth. "Who should mind her own business."

She snickered and rolled her eyes. "Now when has *that* ever happened."

With an exaggerated sigh and a grin pushing his frown, Titus took Jane by the arm and tugged her into the nearest coat closet. Thankfully, it was one of the smaller ones. Close quarters sounded very Christmassy at the moment.

"Sorry about Paige. She likes stories too."

Jane focused her attention on the buttons of his shirt and worried her bottom lip. Neither of them had any space to move except toward each other, a thought that had him pushing a strand of her golden hair back from her cheek. "Jane, I meant what I said back at the inn. This"—he waved a hand between them, and her gaze came back to his— "isn't temporary to me. At least I don't want it to be."

"I don't want it to be temporary either." Her grin peeked from behind the frown.

"And the Christmas invitation still stands."

"I was hoping I'd have a place to stay." Her teeth skimmed over her bottom lip and she slipped a step closer. "Titus, I like the idea of *our* story."

He whistled low and captured her hand in his. "That does have a nice ring to it."

"It sure does." Her smile spread to her eyes. "And just so you know, I have every intention of putting you into my long-term plans."

"I'm usually not a fan of plans, but that one sounds fantastic." He pulled her against him and cupped her cheeks. "But if you place my name into one of those Excel sheets of yours, would you make sure we share a box instead of having separate boxes. I'd feel closer to you if you—"

She stopped his verbal onslaught with a little taste of Pink Ladies, and, oh boy, the flavor was perfect.

"Titus Stewart, I'm pretty sure I'm in love with you."

He kissed her again, buying time to find his voice. Or perhaps just because he liked kissing her. "Jane Cecily, I *know* I'm in love with you."

She ran a palm down his cheek, her emerald eyes shining with tears—happy ones, this time. "That's a wonderful beginning to a story."

ACKNOWLEDGMENTS

Every story has a cast of nonfiction characters who make the fictional characters possible. Here are a few 'thank yous' to the remarkable people who made this story come to life.

To my editor, Marisa Deshaies, who cleaned up this novel under challenging time-constraints. Thank you for your patience and encouragement.

Roseanna White, thanks for partnering with me to make the perfect cover for this fun story.

To my ever-faithful and ever-encouraging Street Team. I love doing this journey with you guys. Thank you for cheering on this story and falling in love with #terrifictitus too. Rachel and Kim, thanks for reading the earliest version of this story and reminding me that it was worth the edits to introduce Titus Stewart to the world.

To the #terrifictrio, Carrie, Beth, and Rachel. Ladies, thank you for constantly talking me off the ledges and reminding me that these stories are worthwhile. I'm thankful God brought you into my life and I get to be a part of yours. Thank you so much.

As always, thanks to my amazing parents who give endless support to me.

I'm blessed to live with an entire family of heroes and am so thankful for the story we write together every day. Love you, Dwight, Ben, Aaron, Lydia, Samuel, and Phoebe.

And to the hero of all heroes, my Savior Jesus Christ. I am so thankful that you hold my story in your hand from beginning to the happily-ever-after. Thank you that *your love is always*.

ABOUT THE AUTHOR

Pepper Basham is an award-winning author who writes romance peppered with grace and humor. She currently resides in the lovely mountains of Asheville, NC where she is the mom of 5 great kids, speech pathologist to about fifty more, lover of chocolate, jazz, and Jesus. Her *Mitchell's Crossroads* series is a reader-favorite and her *Penned in Time* series has garnered national recognition. Her novels *Just the Way You Are* and *The Thorn Healer* released with a 4 1/2 star review from RT and a Top Picks rating. You can learn more about her books at wwwpepperdbasham.com and touch base with her on Facebook, Twitter, or Instagram.

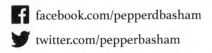

facebook.com/pepperdbasham

twitter.com/pepperbasham

ALSO BY PEPPER D BASHAM

Historical Romance

The Penned in Time Series

The Thorn Bearer

The Thorn Keeper

The Thorn Healer

Historical Romance Novella

Façade

Contemporary Romance

The Mitchell's Crossroads Series

A Twist of Faith

Charming the Troublemaker

A Pleasant Gap Romance

Just the Way You Are

Contemporary Romance Novella

Second Impressions